# DEATH COMES CALLING

Rounding the corner, Slocum saw the deadly scene unwinding in front of him. The man who had pretended to be drunk earlier stopped Stevenson, but Andy kept him at arm's length. Slocum's hand flashed to his hip. He cleared leather fast and brought his Colt Navy up in a practiced movement. His thumb cocked the six-shooter, and his index finger tightened in the same movement. He hardly felt the recoil as the six-gun discharged—and robbed the man behind Stevenson of his life.

Stevenson swung around, startled. He saw the man behind him drop a drawn pistol and then slump to the ground, dead.

Slocum drew a bead on the other man and started to fire. But there was no call for that. The man hightailed it, feet pounding loudly against the ground as he ran.

"Slocum, what's going on?" Andrew Stevenson looked from the dead man to Slocum and then back. "He's dead."

"You'd be the dead one if I hadn't come along." Slocum knelt and picked up the fallen gun. He handed it to Stevenson, who took it in curiously steady hands. The young man still hadn't realized how close death had come to visiting him.

# JAKE LOGAN

## SLOCUM
### AND THE TWO
### GOLD BULLETS

JOVE BOOKS, NEW YORK

**THE BERKLEY PUBLISHING GROUP**
**Published by the Penguin Group**
**Penguin Group (USA) Inc.**
**375 Hudson Street, New York, New York 10014, USA**

Penguin Group (Canada), 90 Eglinton Avenue East, Suite 700, Toronto, Ontario M4P 2Y3, Canada
(a division of Pearson Penguin Canada Inc.)
Penguin Books Ltd., 80 Strand, London WC2R 0RL, England
Penguin Group Ireland, 25 St. Stephen's Green, Dublin 2, Ireland (a division of Penguin Books Ltd.)
Penguin Group (Australia), 250 Camberwell Road, Camberwell, Victoria 3124, Australia
(a division of Pearson Australia Group Pty. Ltd.)
Penguin Books India Pvt. Ltd., 11 Community Centre, Panchsheel Park, New Delhi—110 017, India
Penguin Group (NZ), Cnr. Airborne and Rosedale Roads, Albany, Auckland 1310, New Zealand
(a division of Pearson New Zealand Ltd.)
Penguin Books (South Africa) (Pty.) Ltd., 24 Sturdee Avenue, Rosebank, Johannesburg 2196,
South Africa

Penguin Books Ltd., Registered Offices: 80 Strand, London WC2R 0RL, England

This is a work of fiction. Names, characters, places, and incidents either are the product of the author's imagination or are used fictitiously, and any resemblance to actual persons, living or dead, business establishments, events, or locales is entirely coincidental.

SLOCUM AND THE TWO GOLD BULLETS

A Jove Book / published by arrangement with the author

PRINTING HISTORY
Jove edition / February 2006

ISBN: 0-515-14068-6

JOVE®
Jove Books are published by The Berkley Publishing Group,
a division of Penguin Group (USA) Inc.,
375 Hudson Street, New York, New York 10014.
JOVE is a registered trademark of Penguin Group (USA) Inc.
The "J" design is a trademark belonging to Penguin Group (USA) Inc.

PRINTED IN THE UNITED STATES OF AMERICA

10  9  8  7  6  5  4  3  2  1

# 1

The bright Colorado sun said summer but the cold wind blowing in John Slocum's face whispered winter. He looked around at the vegetation and saw he was getting into the mountains blocking him from easy passage into Utah to the west. Pine and juniper, even aspen and bushes always found at the higher elevations surrounded him. He had ridden along lost in his own thoughts and had hardly noticed the change until now.

He pulled up his collar against the sharp wind blowing down the mountain slope, tugged his hat a little farther down onto his forehead and kept riding. This was a well-travelled road from the look of the double ruts, and whatever town lay ahead would be a good spot to hole up for the night. When his belly growled, he knew he had to take on more supplies, especially if the weather turned suddenly. Slocum sniffed hard at the air but didn't scent or taste snow. Not yet. Soon.

Eventually Slocum reached a spot in the road where the mountains in front of him blocked a modicum of the wind and left only the bright autumn sun on his face. He felt downright good by the time he rode into the small town of Victory. The town might be small but it looked mighty fine

1

to him, especially when he saw narrow-gauge railroad tracks angling away to the north into towering mountains. A train station meant supplies reached Victory on a regular basis, brought down prices and kept the thin wad of greenbacks riding in Slocum's shirt pocket from disappearing entirely.

"Howdy," called a man sitting on a porch in front of a dry goods store, whittling carefully at a length of green pinewood.

Slocum touched the brim of his Stetson and returned a smile. Victory was a right friendly place. Too bad he couldn't stay a spell and sample all its hospitality, but Slocum had caught a disease and it sorely affected him. He had spent almost a month in Denver and now had itchy-foot. Too much of the large city had worn down his temper and set him on the trail again, going somewhere. Mostly, he didn't care where he travelled as long as it was farther down the road.

Still, Victory looked to be a nice little town.

Slocum swung from the saddle, stretched trail-weary muscles, then went into the general store. As he walked around the crowded interior, his quick green eyes took in prices and varieties. He'd been right. Having a train depot kept prices down to the merely outrageous from impossible-to-pay. He scooped canned goods from the neatly stacked shelves, along with a sack of flour, coffee, beans other items that would go good when he got to the other side of the purpled mountains rising to Victory's west.

"You gettin' ready to go out? Got any special place you're headin'?" the proprietor asked, tallying Slocum's purchase.

"Passing through," Slocum said. He was surprised when the man laughed.

"That's what they all say."

"Who do you mean?" Slocum used a burlap bag to collect his canned and dry victuals, then passed across more than half of his poke. Greenbacks wouldn't do him any good out on the trail, but he still hated to spend so much. It had been a long time since he'd seen a payday and the gamblers in Denver knew the odds as good as he did—and handled cards just a mite better.

"The prospectors, that's who," the proprietor said.

"Victory doesn't look like a boomtown," Slocum said. He slung the sack over his shoulder.

"You jist wait, but then I reckon you know all about it." The proprietor gave Slocum a broad wink, as if sharing a secret. Slocum stepped back into the cool afternoon, looking around for a decent place to stay for the night. There was a slightly canted three-story hotel built of red brick, but it had the promise of being expensive since it was close to the train depot. He shrugged the sack into a more comfortable position, grabbed the reins of his horse and walked to the livery stables. It took ten minutes and a bit of dickering but Slocum got a stall for his gelding and some straw for himself to sleep on that night. The livery stable owner was an old geezer, more drunk than sober and taciturn to the point of rudeness. Slocum didn't much care since he wasn't going to be around long enough to make friends. He stashed his gear, then set off to explore Victory.

It took him only a few minutes to gravitate toward the Sweetwater Saloon and Gambling Emporium. The sun dipped low over the mountains he intended to put at his back come the next sunset, and the gathering twilight lent a tad of real chill to the air. Stepping into the smoky, hot saloon was almost a pleasure.

A bored woman worked the box as she dealt faro to one side of the doorway. To the other side stretched three green felt-topped tables. Only one had a poker game in progress. Slocum eyed the gamblers and tried to figure if this was even close to being an honest game.

"What's yer pleasure, mister?" asked the barkeep.

"Beer," Slocum said, fishing out a dime and dropping it

on the bar. He got a mug of surprisingly cold beer and a nickel change. Reaching over to the jar at the end of the bar, he plucked out a pickle and began eating it, wishing he had been here earlier for the free lunch advertised in a small sign stuck in a crack in the wall above the pickle jar.

Slocum leaned back, elbows on the bar and watched the gamblers play a few hands. He had less than four dollars left, but he might augment this pitiful hoard of his into something worth bragging on.

"You ready to go out?" asked the barkeep.

"I'll be riding on in the morning," Slocum said.

"Thought maybe you were here to prospect. You've got the look of a man used to roamin' the high country."

"Gold?" Slocum asked. "Is that what's got everyone so edgy?"

"Hush up," the barkeep said. "Ain't nobody supposed to know about the gold."

Slocum snorted and took another sip of the beer, nursing it. He hadn't been in Victory an hour and already everyone he'd spoken to had broadly hinted at a gold strike. Hinted? He laughed outright this time. The barkeep had done everything but spell it out. Slocum had seen too many towns ruined by the sudden influx of miners, then the equally sudden rush out when gold was discovered elsewhere.

"You know those gents?" Slocum asked, pointing to the gamblers at the table.

"Nope, ain't seen 'em here before. 'Cept for old Kinney. He's a local. They came in on the noon train from Denver. I keep track of such things since I'm the town's mayor." The barkeep puffed out his chest and looked pleased as punch at such a role, especially in light of Victory's newfound prominence as a boomtown.

Slocum pegged the tattered-looking gambler on the far side of the table as Kinney. He had a glassy-eyed stare speaking of too much whiskey that the others took advantage of repeatedly. The three others might be in cahoots or they might be honest gamblers, as far as that went. Slocum had no trouble with cheating gamblers as long as they worked alone. If he had to watch a team at work, the stakes were never worth the risk of being shot in the back because he looked at the wrong player.

One gambler left and sat in on a new game. A man dressed in the rough denims of a prospector filled the empty chair. Soon enough one of the remaining two well-dressed gamblers left. Slocum took his place.

"You need some fresh money in the pot?" he asked. He stared directly at the gambler with the headlight diamond in his tie. The man didn't quite rattle when he moved, but he came close. Slocum saw two knives, a pair of derringers and the obvious six-shooter slung in a shoulder rig. What he didn't see was any kind of mechanism to facilitate cheating. Slocum had seen elaborate devices that snared a high card and then returned it to the gambler's hand later, when it mattered more. But if any cheating went on in this game, it came from card manipulation.

Slocum could handle cheating like that.

The ebb and flow of the game caught Slocum up, and he remembered draining his beer, getting another from a hurdy-gurdy girl and slowly raking in more and more money until he faced the well-dressed gambler across from him. If ever there was a time for a man to cheat, it was now.

Slocum watched like a hawk as the gambler shuffled the cards, then dealt. Peering at his cards, Slocum tried to keep from showing his surprise. He had a full house, deuces over queens. But because of the small, fleeting smirk on the gambler's lips, Slocum turned wary. Betting went slowly.

"How many cards?" asked the gambler, fingering the deck. He started to strip off a few for himself. This told Slocum everything he needed to know. The gambler didn't expect him to draw.

"I'll take two," Slocum said, tossing the queens onto the

table. The shock on the gambler's face was almost as good as winning the pot. Almost.

"Y-you want t-two?"

"Two," Slocum said. "You got a problem with that?"

"T-two," the gambler stuttered, dealing the cards to Slocum. His once sure hands now trembled. Slocum shifted a little in his chair so he could free up the Colt Navy he carried in a cross-draw holster should the need arise.

Slocum hardly glanced at the cards he'd been dealt. Two clubs. He guessed what the rest of the gambler's hand looked like.

"I'll call," Slocum said suddenly. He wanted to be sure.

The gambler turned over three clubs, a heart and a spade. The two clubs Slocum had asked for had ruined the straight flush. He would have bet heavily with a full house, then lost to a flush. With his three deuces, he still won easily.

"Don't," Slocum cautioned as the gambler reached under his coat. The gambler slowly withdrew a handkerchief and mopped his forehead.

"You got me fair and square, mister," the gambler said.

"Nothing fair or square about your dealing."

"I don't want trouble," the gambler said, a slight quaver coming into his voice.

"Congratulations, son," came a hearty voice. Slocum glanced to one side and saw a corpulent man dressed in finery better suited to an opening night at the Denver Opera House.

"We got business," Slocum said, watching the gambler closely.

"No, no we ain't," the gambler said, scuttling from the table. "You got business with Mr. Aiken, I'll let you alone."

"Well, well, seems folks are polite and thoughtful in Victory," the man said, sinking into the chair vacated by the gambler. The wood creaked under the man's bulk.

"The polite ones introduce themselves," Slocum said.

"What? Oh, sorry, so sorry. The name's Aiken. Basil Aiken."

"I've heard of you." Slocum thrust his hand out across the table and introduced himself. Aiken's reaction interested Slocum. The man actually drew back as if being recognized was a bad thing.

"How's that, Mr. Slocum?"

"The barkeep mentioned you when I came in. Said you were a fine, upstanding fellow."

Aiken laughed heartily, his huge belly shaking. "I need to hire him to do publicity for me, then."

Slocum said nothing more after his small fishing expedition. The mayor-bartender had said nothing at all about Aiken, but the thrill of fear that had passed across Aiken's face warned Slocum of something less than legal about the man. Aiken would not have come over the way he had unless he wanted something. What this might be was beyond Slocum's ability to guess.

"You settled in real good. Took a few dollars in a poker game. You're quite the gambler, sir."

"I play the odds," Slocum said carefully.

"You do more than that, unless I miss my guess. You have the look of a man of daring and intelligence about him. You're trailwise, too, I reckon."

"You might say that." Slocum shifted slightly to keep his hand free to go for the ebony-handled six-shooter at his left hip. Something about this hail-fellow-well-met greeting didn't sit well with him. Aiken didn't have the look of a man who did his own dirty work, and he certainly would not try to steal the money Slocum had won, not in a public place like the Sweetwater Saloon, now filled to overflowing with men all shouting out their orders for whiskey and beer. But Aiken wanted something.

"I need a decent scout. You've worked as a scout, haven't you? Perhaps for the Army?"

"I've scouted," Slocum said.

"You're the man I need, then!" Aiken slammed his open hand down on the table and caused the empty beer mugs to jump about. He leaned forward, as if forcing himself to control his enthusiasm and whispered conspiratorially, "Gold. The hills are gravid with gold, sir. And I need you to take one of my surveyors out to claim it."

"That's it? Who's the surveyor you want me to scout for?"

"My right-hand man, he is. Name of Andrew Stevenson. A good man. A fine man," Aiken said too forcefully.

"I don't think so. I'm just passing through. Wish you the best of luck finding the gold—"

"I know it's here, Mr. Slocum," Aiken said. "It's a matter of getting it registered legally and bringing in miners to work the claim. I'll offer you fifty dollars a week to ride for me."

Slocum flipped through the coins and few bills he had just won in the poker game. It hardly amounted to fifty dollars, and here Aiken offered this much for a simple week of riding, studying the lay of the land, doing things he did anyway for free.

"That's mighty generous. Why so much?"

"It's only a week or two of work for you, I'm afraid, sir, but it has to be done fast. And you, being a newcomer to Victory and all, are perfect. You don't have any allegiances to hold you back."

"You saying people you might hire locally would try to do you out of the gold?"

Aiken coughed genteelly then looked up and smiled. Slocum had never seen such cunning in wide-set brown eyes before.

"When there's this much gold at stake, I'm not sure I would trust my own mother."

Slocum pondered this for a moment. Aiken wouldn't trust his own blood but he would hire a drifter he didn't know from Adam. That didn't make a whole lot of sense, and as rich as the reward for a little scouting work might be, Slocum decided to pass on it. Before he could tell Aiken his decision, the man reared back in his chair and called to the barkeep for a bottle of whiskey.

"We need to celebrate," Aiken said.

"There's nothing to celebrate," Slocum said.

"There's Stevenson now. Andy! Come on over. This is John Slocum and he'll be your guide to . . . the spot."

"Pleased to meet you," Stevenson said. He was an eager young man, maybe in his mid-twenties, with tousled blond hair and an honest enough face weathered by wind and sun. His grip was firm and his hand calloused. Unlike Basil Aiken, Slocum took a liking to Stevenson. But not enough to hire on.

Something just wasn't right.

"Here you are, gentlemen," said the hurdy-gurdy girl, putting the bottle on the table and dropping three shot glasses. Slocum decided there wasn't anything wrong with sampling some of Billy Taylor's Finest Whiskey. To his surprise, it went down smooth and might have actually come all the way from Kentucky in an original bottle. It might have come from Aiken's personal supply.

"When can we leave? I'm real anxious, Mr. Slocum," Stevenson said. "The sooner we get things squared away, the quicker we can get down to the real work."

"Counting our money!" Aiken laughed at his little joke. Stevenson joined in. Slocum took another drink. It was free and all he had to do was listen a bit longer before saying no.

"You got that right, Mr. Aiken," Stevenson said, all puppy-dog eager.

"Is that all right with you? You can leave in the morning?" Aiken eyed Slocum closely.

Slocum balanced his chance of getting another shot of the smooth bourbon whiskey before saying "no" but hesitated. Peering in the saloon door was about the prettiest filly he had set eyes on in a month of Sundays. That she didn't enter told him a great deal about her.

"What? Oh, wait a minute, will you?" Stevenson jumped to his feet and went to the door, spoke a few minutes, then came back. Slocum locked eyes with the lovely woman. She smiled boldly for a lady too well-mannered to enter a drinking emporium, batted her long eyelashes at him, then vanished into the night.

"Sorry for the interruption," Stevenson said.

"Who was that?" Slocum asked, trying to keep his voice level. "Your missus?"

"His wife? That's a rich one!" Aiken laughed even more, having to hold his quaking belly. "No, Mr. Slocum, that's his sister."

"Your sister?"

"Daisy is a sweet girl. When we get rich, I'm going to show her the best time ever back in Denver. That's where we came from. Denver."

Slocum ran his finger around the rim of the shot glass, then licked the drop of whiskey he had captured.

"Sunrise soon enough to hit the trail?" Slocum asked.

# 2

Slocum waited impatiently for Andy Stevenson to show up. The sun had crept above the mountains far to the east almost a half hour earlier. He lounged back and watched as the young stableman went about his chores.

"You been in Victory very long?" Slocum asked.

"What's that? Oh, no," the man said. He continued pitching hay into the center of the stable, getting breakfast ready for the horses waiting as impatiently as Slocum. "Just got to town a month or so back and Smitty—he's the owner—gave me a job. Came up from New Mexico when I heard-tell of a gold strike."

Slocum had to laugh. Everyone knew of the gold strike and yet everyone pretended it was a deep, dark secret. If anything, the real mystery was why Victory hadn't exploded at the seams with prospectors rushing in to become millionaires overnight.

"You decided to feed horses rather than dig gold out of the ground?"

"Something like that," the stableman said. "Actually, I talked it out with Smitty. He's seen 'em come, 'nd seen 'em go. He says the only ones who made any money were the ones who worked hard—at tendin' the prospectors. I thought on it and decided he was right. For an old drunk, Smitty's not so dumb."

"You're a smart man," Slocum said, getting an appreciative grin in response.

"There you are," came Stevenson's aggrieved words. "I thought we were meeting in front of the Sweetwater."

"Figured you had to fetch your horse, so here I am." Slocum said nothing about also sleeping here.

"Let's go, then. I'm in a big hurry. Mr. Aiken said we could get to the spot, survey it and be back before sundown."

"Must not be too far off," Slocum said, leading his horse from its stall. He made certain the girth was screwed down tight. This gelding had a tendency to swell itself up, then exhale and send an inexperienced rider tumbling, saddle and all.

"Here's the map, sir." Stevenson passed over a scrap of paper that had been folded so many times that it was falling apart. Slocum took the paper, gingerly turned it about until he got the compass rose aimed in the right direction, then studied it.

"You're right. The spot marked isn't that far off. Wonder why nobody's found the gold before now?" Slocum scratched his chin, the stubble poking into his work-hardened hand.

"Victory's a new town. Well, not real new," Stevenson said. "The railroad's only been here a few months. General Palmer cut the ribbon here and everything."

Slocum looked at Andy Stevenson and wondered if he was this enthusiastic about everything. He bubbled over with energy as he rose and settled in the saddle repeatedly, anxious to get on the trail. Slocum folded the crude map and tucked it into his shirt pocket.

"Might explain it, but this part of Colorado's been pretty well explored over the last few years, thanks to the fighting with the Utes."

"Oh, there's no Indian trouble now," Stevenson solemnly assured him. "Chief Ouray's promised that, and he's an honorable man."

"I've heard that said of him," Slocum allowed. "Still, there're a few firebrands up north who don't cotton much to his peaceable ways."

"We're here, and we're going to be rich," Stevenson said.

They rode in silence for a few minutes before Slocum worked up his nerve.

"That woman last night. The one who poked her head into the saloon. That's really your sister?"

"Certainly is," Stevenson said proudly. "Daisy's a fine girl."

"Right good-looking one, too," Slocum said. For the first time Stevenson turned and glared, as if warning Slocum to keep his distance.

"Your folks from around this area?"

"It's just me and Daisy," the young man said. "Cholera took our folks. The rest of our people, too. Danged near eighteen Stevensons died in the span of two months last summer."

"Sorry to hear that," Slocum said. "Does Daisy work for Aiken, too?"

"Odd jobs," Stevenson said. "Not like me. Mr. Aiken said it last night. I'm his right-hand man."

Slocum pointed to a game trail leading westward off the main road and let Stevenson fall in behind as they rode single file for a mile, gaining altitude rapidly and entering more rugged, rockier territory. Slocum kept a sharp eye out for any trouble, but the countryside was as quiet here as it was noisy around Victory. They disturbed some wildlife, mostly marmots, and the sight of a fat buck rabbit made Slocum's belly growl. He had skipped breakfast, thinking Stevenson would be early and eager to get on the trail. Instead of taking a shot at the quick rabbit, he reached back into his saddlebags and pulled out some venison jerky. He offered a piece to Stevenson, who hesitated, then shook his head.

"You can scrape off the green fuzz. It's not so old yet that it'll kill you," Slocum said, biting down on the tough meat and chewing methodically, letting his saliva soften it before swallowing. Even then, it went down hard and caught about halfway down his swallow pipe. He took a long pull from his canteen and this washed the reluctant jerky all the way to his belly. Although he had fresher food he had bought in Victory, he wanted to finish what he already had. Waste not, want not.

"Thanks, but I'm too excited to eat. I've never been this close to being rich before."

"This gold find? It'd be yours?"

"Oh, no, it's Mr. Aiken's since he found it and is putting up the money to exploit it and—"

"How's he know there's anything out here?" Slocum looked around. He was no geologist but had some experience when it came to finding gold. The rock in these parts might be good for something, but finding gold in them wasn't one of them. Not like up in California Gulch or around Cripple Creek. The rock here looked like . . . rock.

"He—I don't know," admitted the young man. "He's struck it rich before, so he knows 'bout all there is when it comes to gold mining."

"Do tell," Slocum said. He wasn't much impressed with the way this hunt for blue dirt went. A small stream meandered down from higher ground but nothing caught his eye in the small pools of water. Not so much as a golden glimmer to show there might be flakes of the precious metal here.

"Is this the area?"

"Could be. Hard to tell from the map," Slocum said. Stevenson pulled out a notebook and a stub of a pencil and began scribbling frantically. Now and then, like a chicken taking a break from pecking at grain, the young man looked around, then went back to his frantic writing. Slocum had no idea what had impressed Stevenson so mightily that he had to record it.

"Is this spot known to anyone else?"

"How could it be? Mr. Aiken is the only one who knows about it. Him and us, that is. Why do you ask?"

"Somebody's come this way recently," Slocum said, shielding his eyes against the bright Colorado sun as he studied the muddy area around the pond where he had first looked for specks of gold. At least four riders had watered their mounts here. Their deep hoofprints in the mud had filled but were still visible, leading Slocum to believe the riders were gone only a half hour or so.

He looked around, then caught sight of a few broken twigs on a shrub. He pointed them out to Stevenson.

"What's it mean?" Everything the young man said reinforced Slocum's belief that this was as close to roughing it as he had ever gotten. Since Stevenson was such a tenderfoot, that meant Daisy Stevenson was the product of a city, too. That set Slocum thinking in other directions, mostly about Daisy Stevenson, but he shook his head to clear his thoughts. This was no time to lose concentration, not with a band of unidentified riders nearby.

"From the direction the bigger limbs are bent and the twigs broken, they went uphill. Might be they're on the ridge now, watching us."

"No, they can't. They can't know about the gold."

"There's no gold here," Slocum said irritably.

"You said this was the spot marked on the map."

"It is," Slocum said, "but I don't see any gold." He reached over and slid the leather keeper off the hammer of his Colt Navy. It was quiet. The riders might have travelled on and could be halfway to Cortez by now, but a cold knot formed in his gut that told him different.

"I need to put out stone markers."

"You get your survey equipment out and tend to the mapping," Slocum said. "I'll scout up there."

"Equipment?"

Slocum swung in the saddle and stared at Stevenson. The young man was genuinely puzzled.

"Aiken said you were going to survey the area. You need equipment for that."

"I . . . I don't have anything like that. I was only going to put up stone markers—piles of rock. And record it." Stevenson held up his notebook as if this explained everything.

Slocum shook his head.

"You stay here. Don't stray far."

"What's wrong? You know something you're not telling me."

"Don't go drawing any attention to yourself. Water your horse, then go set yourself down under that tree." Slocum pointed out the one affording the best cover. "You don't want to take too much sun."

Stevenson started to protest, then clamped his mouth shut and looked a tad petulant. Slocum ignored the reaction. The feeling of something being seriously wrong grew. He itched to draw the Winchester from its sheath and lever a round into the chamber, just in case. But he rode slowly along the same path taken by the earlier band, every sense alert. He heard Andy Stevenson grumbling back at the shallow pool along the stream, and he ignored him so he could concentrate on other, smaller sounds. Wind through the aspen leaves, through the pine needles. The sound of a distant animal thrashing about in the brush. A deer? Slocum paid it no attention. Ahead he heard the soft nickering of a horse.

He rode, back straight, eyes ahead and knew now what he was getting himself into. Any show of fear would mean his immediate death.

A grim smile came to his lips. Even if he showed no

fear, he might be killed. Turning and running, even a cautious retracing of his route this far, might result in instant death.

The glint of sunlight off the front sights of a rifle alerted him to the sniper on his left. He heard movement in the brush to his right; this was intended to draw his attention away from the Indians working their way into an ambush ahead, just under the ridge line.

Slocum drew rein and leaned forward, so his hand rested near the butt of his Colt Navy. He did not grab for the six-shooter but wanted to be more than halfway to it if things turned nasty.

"Greetings," Slocum called. He shifted into Shoshone, which was close enough to what the local Weeminuche Ute spoke to get by.

"We speak English," came the angry reply.

"Better than I speak your language," Slocum said.

"You are on Ute land. Get off!"

"Didn't know this was yours," Slocum said. "Fact is, by treaty your land's a ways to the north. You hunting? Game is mighty scarce farther north, I hear."

"This is our land."

"I saw a deer a mile or so back," Slocum went on, ignoring the man who stepped into plain view. The others with him remained hidden. Slocum felt the hair on the back of his neck prickling. The others were hunters and all had their rifles trained on him.

"You do not ride alone. Why did the other remain at the river?"

"Thirsty," Slocum said. "He was mighty thirsty from our ride." He considered lying, saying that they were scouting for a much larger group but knew the Utes weren't likely to buy that for a second. If anything, it might spook them into killing him and Stevenson before hightailing it. Better to palaver for a while. Didn't cost anything and the Ute leader didn't seem inclined to open fire. Not yet.

"More white eyes come to our land."

"Reckon that's true," Slocum said. He saw the surprise on the Indian's face. "A whole bunch of white folks are moving in, according to the treaty your Chief Ouray signed back in Washington."

"Ouray," the brave spat. "He rides in a fine carriage and forgets what it is like to hunt. The Great Father gives Ouray everything he wants. We starve!"

"Sounds like your beef is with your chief," Slocum said. "Not me. Not us. And your land is farther north about twenty miles."

The brave gestured and six other Utes magically appeared. Slocum had a good idea where three had been. The other three were too well hidden to be seen. Seeing how many he faced, he was glad he hadn't shot first and parleyed later.

"You do not fear us."

"You're wrong. I do. But it's no good to go screaming and shouting about it." Slocum again surprised the brave with his frankness. "If you want to bag that deer I saw, you'd better get after it. Mule deer." He hadn't seen any deer, only heard what he thought might be a deer foraging in the undergrowth, but this little lie went further now that the Utes had him pegged as a man who spoke the truth.

"You have gift?"

"For a great warrior such as yourself, I certainly do," Slocum said. He slowly reached down and drew the knife sheathed in his right boot top. A quick flip brought the blade into his palm. He held it out, every movement precise and slow. "For you. To skin that deer."

The brave walked over, looked down his long roman nose at the knife, then took it. A single quick nod was all the acknowledgment Slocum got.

The hunting party backed away and then faded like mist in the morning sun, leaving Slocum alone on his horse, the clear blue Colorado sky stretching above and the rocky, sparsely forested land all around. He sat for a spell, wanting to let out a deep sigh of relief but knowing the Indians might still be watching to see what he did. After a suitable length of time, showing he was neither frightened nor hunting anything in particular in this area, he turned his horse's face and walked slowly back downhill to where Stevenson sat in the shade, obviously fuming.

"What's going on?" the young man demanded.

"Nothing," Slocum said. They had escaped having their scalps lifted, or at least their horses and supplies stolen, but he saw no reason to burden Stevenson with the details. "You got what you need?"

"I put up the stone pyramids. There, there and way over there." He pointed out the knee-high piles of rock. Slocum thought they were piss-poor boundary markers, but he was past caring. All he wanted now was to wet his whistle with some decent bourbon at the Sweetwater Saloon.

"Then let's get on back to Victory and report our success," Slocum said.

This prompted Stevenson to more speed than Slocum had seen him display all day. The man vaulted into the saddle and cantered off. Slocum followed at a more sedate pace, but he thought hard all the way back into Victory. Not much made any sense to him, but as long as Basil Aiken paid him, Slocum decided nothing much had to make sense.

It was well past sunset when they dismounted and tethered their horses in front of the saloon where Aiken made his headquarters. The Sweetwater was noisy tonight, packed almost to overflowing. A piano player hammered away with more gusto than skill, but no one took notice of that. The men were busy dancing with the few women employed by the saloon, and the barkeep worked double-time to keep beer mugs and shot glasses filled. If he was half as diligent being mayor, there was nothing wrong at all in Victory.

"Come on over," called Aiken with what Slocum felt to be forced bonhomie. "You're just in time to help me drink this bottle of whiskey!"

Slocum pulled up a chair and let Aiken pour him a drink.

"Well? How'd it go, boys?" demanded Aiken.

"Andy can tell you everything," Slocum said, wanting to hear what the young man had to offer his boss in the way of tall tales. As far as he could tell, they had accomplished nothing—except almost getting themselves killed by a band of hungry Ute hunters.

"Yes, sir, it's like you said. Slocum found the place right off, and I put up markers as you told me. Here. Here's my notes on what I saw and did."

Aiken glanced at the notebook Stevenson pushed across the table, but Slocum could tell by the way the man's eyes darted around that he wasn't reading the crabbed handwriting. A broad smile crossed the corpulent man's face and he burst out with an ear-splitting cheer that brought a sudden silence to the saloon.

"Gents, let me be the first to announce. We've found gold! There's gold up there in the hills and we found it!"

A thunderous roar built, filled the room and then burst outward to echo from one end of Victory to the other. Slocum leaned back in his chair, sipping the fine whiskey and wondering what the hell was going on.

# 3

Slocum considered riding on after putting away a good breakfast—until he saw Daisy Stevenson talking with her brother. They stood in front of the Sweetwater Saloon in animated conversation. The way the sunlight caught the woman's brilliant blond hair made Slocum think this might be the only worthwhile gold in the area. He heaved a sigh and started to mount to leave Victory, then Daisy turned just a little and he caught her full profile. He sucked in his breath, thought on the money Aiken had promised him to scout, then dismounted. There were more reasons to stay in town, for a while, than there were to leave.

Daisy Stevenson was a big reason to remain. For a while.

He strolled over, taking in her loveliness as he went. She wore a calico skirt with a crisp starched white blouse that strained in the front. If she was any better endowed, those buttons would pop right off. In spite of such obvious charms, though, Slocum found himself staring at her face. No angel had ever been graced with such beauty. Her oval face was perfection in itself, and her bright blue eyes rivalled the clear sky above. She turned a little more, saw him and smiled. That smile alone was worth staying in Victory.

For a while.

"Good morning, Mr. Slocum," she greeted. "How are you this great day?"

"Fine as frog's fur," he assured her.

"We're all floating on clouds," Andy Stevenson said.

"Why's that?" Slocum knew why he felt good. He had a belly filled with decent, well-cooked victuals and had about the prettiest filly in all Colorado smiling at him.

"The gold!" exclaimed Stevenson. "What else could there be?"

"What else," he said, his green eyes locked on Daisy's blue ones. She boldly stared at him, as she had the night before, then averted her eyes. A slight blush came to her cheeks, doing the impossible. It made the young woman look even lovelier.

"I've got to go get ready," Stevenson said. He bent over and kissed Daisy's cheek, then rushed away. At the far end of town hammers pounded fiercely and men worked to put up red, white and blue bunting.

"What's going on?" Slocum asked. "Down there?" He jerked his thumb over his shoulder in the direction the woman's brother had gone.

"Oh, Mr. Aiken is preparing to make the big announcement of the gold strike. It's so rich!" She clapped her hands in glee and bounced up and down as joy seized her anew.

"There's no gold," Slocum said. For a moment he didn't think Daisy heard him. Then she turned fully to him and looked stricken.

"What are you saying?"

"That place your brother marked doesn't have the sort of rock where you'd expect to find gold. I looked in the pools on the stream and didn't see any flecks of gold washed down from higher ground, either."

"But Andy said you took him right to the spot on the map."

"I did, but I'm saying there's no gold to be found."

"Oh, you're funning me. That's it, isn't it, Mr. Slocum?"

Slocum started to explain and then saw it would do no good. It was like arguing religion with a preacher. The words might get heated, they might even carry a kernel of truth, but nothing shook faith. Daisy Stevenson had faith, and it was in the presence of gold where her brother—and Basil Aiken—had said.

"You read me too good, Miss Stevenson," he said, giving in to the inevitable.

"Please, call me Daisy."

"And I'm John."

"Well, John, this is a special day for other reasons."

"I can agree to that," he said, then realized they probably weren't talking about the same thing. Seeing her so close, a hint of perfume making his nostrils flare, he felt his day get brighter. "But what's your good news?"

"It's Andy's, actually," she said. "The stage they're building at the end of town?" She pointed in the direction of the carpenters still hard at work. "Mr. Aiken is going to give him a special reward."

"What might that be? Something equal to him finding so much gold?" Slocum's sarcasm fell on deaf ears. Daisy was too excited to hear anything but what she wanted.

"It surely must be a fine reward," Daisy said.

"May I escort you?" Slocum asked, extending his arm. Daisy smiled even more broadly and locked her arm through his. Arm-in-arm they walked the length of Victory's main street and found a spot on the boardwalk where they were out of the hot autumn sun and could see the platform Aiken had ordered built.

"That's Andy," the blonde said proudly. "Ma and Pa never figured he'd amount to a hill of beans. Look at him now."

"Sitting up there with a . . . mine owner," Slocum said dubiously.

"He's found some of the biggest strikes in Colorado," Daisy said.

"Has he now? Such as?"

"Why, Mr. Aiken developed the Golden Lamb in the Front Range west of Denver, then moved over the Rockies and worked the Silly Goose and Lady's Lament mines when everyone else thought they'd petered out."

"I've heard of them," Slocum said, dredging up old memories. "I've heard of the Golden Lamb. That's Aiken's?"

"It certainly is," Daisy said, as proud as if she owned it herself.

Slocum felt a pang of doubt creep into his cynical expectations of Basil Aiken. A faint memory crept up that a man named Aiken had found a mine where no one else would bother looking, and that it had been extremely rich.

"Ladies and gentlemen, citizens of the fine town of Victory!" called Aiken. He thrust out his chest and let his belly bounce just a bit under a fancy brocade vest with its dangling gold watch chain and small medallion signifying his membership in the Fraternal Order of the Moose. "This is a stellar day for us all. My good friend and associate, Mr. Andrew Stevenson, has discovered one of the richest veins of gold ore in the entire state of Colorado. And believe me, I know rich!"

A low murmur turned into applause and cheers.

"And believe me when I say I am going to make you all rich—through Andy's discovery of gold in the hills to the west of town. The La Plata Mountains will ring with the sound of picks and blasting—and wagons rattling away laden with blocks of solid gold because there won't be enough railroad freight cars for so much wealth!"

"He knows how to keep a crowd's attention," Slocum said.

"Hush. He's getting to the reward," Daisy said. She clung to his arm. In spite of the warmth of the day, Slocum found he didn't mind at all. Daisy was the prettiest woman in town by several dozen rows of apple trees.

"I do not award this readily," Aiken roared. He held up something that glittered gold in the sunlight. "It is a prize that must be earned through meritorious service. I am proud to say that Mr. Stevenson has earned my personal golden bullet!"

Slocum got a better look at it as Aiken held it between thumb and index finger, turning slowly to show it to everyone in the crowd. Then he handed it to Stevenson, clasped the young man to his ample chest and gave him a hearty slap on the back.

"He's clever, he's got a nose for gold, and he works for me!"

This produced a new round of laughter and applause.

"Mr. Stevenson, please show the ladies and gents in the audience your golden bullet. And while you're down there mingling with them, let them know how they can be part of this extraordinary venture."

"What's he mean?" asked Slocum.

"This is an honor," Daisy said, almost breathless with excitement. "Not only did he give Andy a gold bullet, he's letting him sell stock certificates in the mine."

"Don't crowd him, my good people. There are plenty of shares in the newly named Mother Lode Mine to go around!"

"I hope Andy gets lots and lots of shares," Daisy said. "It'll make us rich."

Slocum started to remind her that he had been with her brother and had seen no trace of gold at the spot where Aiken declared the Mother Lode Mine to be brimming with precious metal. He bit his lip to hold back the words because she thought he had been pulling her leg when he had said so before.

Slocum and Daisy waited until the furor died down and Stevenson made his way to where they stood. The young man was flushed and out of breath with excitement.

"I've sold a thousand shares already! Look!"

"Don't flash that around," Slocum said, pushing down

the young man's hand clutching a wad of greenbacks.
Stevenson's pockets bulged with coins and more scrip
threatening to come tumbling out.

"It's all right, John," Daisy said. "Nobody's going to
steal the money. The townspeople know how much we're
all in this together."

"What's he paying you?" Slocum asked bluntly.

"Mr. Aiken? Why, I'm taking my salary in stock certificates. They're only a buck apiece now, but when the gold
starts pouring out of the Mother Lode Mine they'll be
worth thousands of dollars each. We're gonna be rich,
Daisy, richer than you ever thought."

"How much?" repeated Slocum.

"He's paying me a hundred dollars a week . . ."

"In gold mining stock certificates," Slocum finished. Andrew Stevenson bobbed his head up and down in agreement.

"Come on, Daisy. Let's celebrate. I'll buy you the best
damn lunch they have in that restaurant in the hotel."

"Andy, don't swear." Daisy lowered her eyes but gave
Slocum a sidelong glance, as if wanting him to join them.

"If I'm going to keep up with your brother, I'd better get
to work myself," Slocum said.

"See you later, John?" The way Daisy said it was less a
question than a statement, more a lewd suggestion than a
simple acknowledgment.

"Count on it," Slocum said. Daisy brushed past him, her
hand lingering slightly as she touched his arm. Then she
and her brother went off, cheerfully greeting people stopping occasionally for Andy to sell a few shares in the
Mother Lode Mine.

Slocum stepped back and watched Basil Aiken working
his way through the crowd, also selling stock certificates in
his mine. After a few minutes, Aiken gave up and the
hangers-on drifted away. He smoothed his vest, adjusted
his top hat to a jaunty angle and set off down the street. At
first Slocum thought Aiken might be joining his assistant

and Daisy at the restaurant but Aiken kept walking, finally turning into the general store. On impulse, Slocum followed briskly, slowed and then swung around to sit in a chair by the door next to a large pickle barrel. Tipping the chair back, Slocum pulled down his hat and turned his head slightly so he could hear what went on inside the store between Aiken and the proprietor.

". . . going jist as you said, Mr. Aiken," the owner said. "I'm sure glad you loaned me so much money to order more stock from Denver."

"You're a wise man, Rupert," Aiken said. "Although I had to advance you the money at such a large interest rate, you'll make more in the long run selling supplies."

"Got a whole shipment of picks, shovels and other mining equipment comin' in on the train. Ought to be here in a day or two."

"Excellent. You are going to become quite rich, Rupert, rich beyond your dreams because you understand the economics of a gold rush."

"Uh, Mr. Aiken?"

"Yes, Rupert?"

"You got any more of them stock certificates left? I'm making a young fortune off sellin' to folks, but I want to make *real* money."

"By owning a share or two in the Mother Lode Mine? You are in luck. I happen to have one more certificate right here in the pocket next to my heart."

Slocum peered inside and saw how eagerly the proprietor shoved over a sheaf of money in exchange for the stock certificate. He quickly swung around and pulled his hat down to hide his face as Aiken left, stopped at the edge of the boardwalk, stretched mightily and went to the Sweetwater Saloon. Slocum waited for the mining magnate to go inside before following. It took Aiken more than twenty minutes to make his way to the bar and order some whiskey because he was so busy selling more shares in his nonexistent mine. More interesting to Slocum was the business dealing Aiken had with the barkeep.

Aiken owned a minority interest in the saloon, arranging for a distillery in Denver to ship whiskey straight to the Sweetwater's back room.

Slocum watched as Aiken entered more than a half dozen businesses—including the bakery, the apothecary's shop, even a bookstore—making loans as he went. While the exact amounts weren't stated, Aiken might own most of Victory.

He owned most of Victory and sold shares in a gold mine that might not have so much as a fleck of metal in it.

Slocum had no reason to care but found himself worrying that Daisy and her brother were caught up in the middle of what could be a scam. Since they seemed oblivious to the deals Aiken wrangled, they were probably being duped as much—more!—than the rest of the citizens in Victory.

Slocum went to the stables, saddled his horse and mounted. He made sure he had supplies for several days in his saddlebags and started out.

"Hey, Mr. Slocum," called the young stableman, "you gonna be gone long?"

"Don't rightly know. A day or two. Why?"

"Smitty tells me I can rent that stall, if you're not boardin' your horse. He's expectin' a whole passel of prospectors comin' into town now that gold's been found." In spite of what he had said before, the young man looked pained that he was talking about stabling a horse and not where the best place to make his own claim might be.

Slocum had paid for a week in advance. The stableman was going to get twice his usual fee. Slocum didn't care. Compared to what he thought Aiken was up to, this was an honest scheme.

"Back in a day or two. Go on, rent it out, but I'll want it when I get back."

"Thanks!"

Slocum rode from Victory, going past the newly built platform where Aiken had presented his special golden bullet to an appreciative Andy Stevenson.

Once out of town Slocum felt the familiar rush of freedom and considered not returning, but he felt he owed something to Daisy and her gullible brother. Aiken worked a swindle and had involved them in it. Slocum needed some proof before taking evidence to the town marshal and getting Stevenson out of trouble before it became too late.

It was especially important to get solid evidence of a flimflam because Daisy had sparked his memory. Basil Aiken *had* operated the Golden Lamb and the other mines farther north, bringing out prodigious amounts of gold from the bowels of the earth. This knowledge caused Slocum a pang of doubt; why would a man who was rolling in gold dust want to bamboozle the gullible people in a small town like Victory? Slocum had no idea. Aiken had already pocketed hundreds, if not thousands, of dollars selling the stock certificates to the Mother Lode Mine and had his thumb in every other business pie in town, but Aiken was already a millionaire. What were a paltry few extra dollars to him?

This, as much as any obligation Slocum felt to Daisy and Andrew, kept him riding back to the spot Stevenson had staked out the Mother Lode Mine claim.

It was well past midnight by the time Slocum got to the site. He pitched camp, fixed some dinner and then turned in for the night, to get an early start poking around the area, but dawn did not awaken him. What sounded like horses passing in the predawn hours did. Slocum sat up, hand wrapped around his Colt Navy. The sound of hooves faded, going toward higher ground.

Slocum shook off the cold and felt more than a hint of early winter in the air. He poked at the campfire embers and coaxed a small blaze, which he fed with more twigs until he had enough of a cooking fire to boil some coffee. Two cups of the strong Arbuckle's Fine Coffee brought him entirely awake.

Stretching his cramped muscles, Slocum stood, broke camp and rode slowly to where Stevenson had placed the first marker. By now dawn lit the sky with pale pinks and the promise of even more illumination in a few minutes. Slocum poked around, looking carefully at the rocks Stevenson had used. Nothing worthy of note. He went to the pond and sloshed about, using the rising sun to see if any gold flecks reflected at the bottom of the pool. Nothing but fool's gold.

An hour more search of the area turned up nothing Slocum recognized as gold-bearing ore. No blue dirt, no lead carbonate that might hint at silver. Nothing. He worked his way toward the steeper slope to check outcroppings. By midday he was a mile off and examining a sheer face of stone rising more than thirty feet. If a vein of ore rambled through the mountain it might come out on this flat expanse.

Slocum dug a handpick from his saddlebags and began chipping away diligently. After ten minutes, Slocum stepped back and wiped sweat from his forehead, then hesitated. Something alerted him to look up in time to see a huge rock plummeting down from above. Slocum moved fast to get out of the way—but not fast enough.

Sharp pain lanced through his head and then the world went black.

# 4

Slocum hoped he wasn't dead. If he was, death hurt too damned much. He tried to force himself to hands and knees but couldn't move. He collapsed flat on his belly and lay on the ground, crushed by rock on his back. He wiggled about a little more, got his head turned so his nose caught a hint of fresh, dust-free air. He sucked in huge drafts until his strength returned. He continued to wiggle like a snake and finally worked a hand free so he could wipe the dirt and grit off his face and clear his eyes.

For a heart-stopping instant he thought he was blind, then he realized it was night. A star or two burned through the mist that still obscured his vision. Shaking and shivering, he moved and struggled to get more rock off him until only one large rock pinned him to the ground. He succeeded in turning onto his side and getting out from under. The cessation of pressure caused a deep gasp to escape his lips. From this point it was only a matter of minutes before he was completely free of the rockfall and sitting with his back to the sheer wall rising to the nighttime sky.

He wiped more at his eyes and finally cleared his vision entirely. Slocum stared at the last rock he had escaped from under and let out a low whistle. He had missed being crushed to death through blind luck. A huge rock had tumbled from above but it had wedged itself between two others. Its prodigious weight had broken the supporting rocks but that had robbed the rock of its deadly power, merely pinning Slocum rather than smashing him to a pulp. He rubbed his hands over his back and arms. His fingers came away bloody from the scratches, but when he stood and stretched he didn't feel anything broken. More than one twinge made him wince, but he was alive.

Stepping away from the cliff face, he looked up to see if he could spot where an outcrop of rock had broken free. In the dark, he couldn't make out where the small avalanche had started or what had triggered it. With his inability to spot the source came the determination to climb to the top of the cliff to inspect it—and as quickly came a weakness in his legs. Slocum staggered a few steps, then sat heavily.

It was time for him to get back to town.

He whistled for his horse but no answering whinny came. Slocum called out but his voice was swallowed by the night. He craned his neck around and looked at the stars. He had been pinned under the rockfall for better than two hours. Cursing, Slocum got to his feet and went to find where his horse had wandered off to.

Less than a minute later, he found how badly he had maligned the animal's devotion. He found the right rear leg poking out from under an even larger rock than the one that had almost stolen away his life. A bit of digging revealed the rest of the horse's body. Slocum worked methodically, if a bit clumsily, and got his gear free of the dead horse. He dropped his saddle and collapsed onto it, intending to rest for a few minutes. Instead, exhaustion seized him and he came closer to passing out than to sleeping. Slocum awoke around noon, the sun burning down into his face. Rolling to his side, then to his belly for a giddy moment, Slocum finally forced himself to his feet. Dizziness hit him like a hammer, but he remained erect. He slung his saddlebags over his shoulder, got his bearings and started back in the direction of Victory.

Every step wore on him, but Slocum doggedly kept moving. He knew from the way his head felt like it would split open at any instant that he had jumbled up his brains, but to remain out in the mountains was a sure death warrant. He would die alone. That thought came to obsess him as he walked. He had to get help. Doctor in Victory. Somewhere.

Well past sundown Slocum realized he heard voices, followed quickly by gunfire. His hand went to the Colt holstered at his side, but his hand was too weak to properly clutch the butt. But that didn't matter. The voices turned to laughter and more gunshots suggested miners having a good time, not men dying.

"Victory," Slocum thought, staggering on. He was close to town. He was close to getting help.

"John? Is that you? Whatever happened?"

Slocum almost recognized the voice. He turned and looked around but saw no one. His eyes refused to properly focus as he dropped to his knees.

"John!"

"Who's there?" he croaked out. He hadn't drunk anything all day. No water, the exertion, the rocks bouncing off his head and back, all conspired to do him in. But the voice was a heavenly angel's. "Am I dead?"

"Damn near," the voice said. "Tell me what happened. Never mind. Come along."

He felt gentle hands that turned stronger when it became obvious he could not move under his own power without considerable help. Slocum's vision blurred a mite as he tried to focus on where they were heading, then he gave in to the inevitable and let Daisy take him wherever she wanted. As they staggered along, her arm supporting a good bit of his weight, he decided that wasn't a bad thing. Not bad at all.

"Here we are," Daisy said, opening a door and letting

him half-stumble into a small shack. The outside might
have been decrepit but he saw the inside had been done up
just fine. There were even curtains over the single window
on the far wall, just above a bed.

"Your place?" he asked. Slocum tried to swallow and
found his mouth filled with cotton. He sank down onto the
bed and tried to remain upright. It was a struggle but
worth it. He saw Daisy turn, bend over and fetch a dipper-
ful of water for him. She handed him the water, watching
him intently.

"You're quite a faker, aren't you?"

Slocum swallowed the water, some of it spilling down
his shirt in his hurry to get as much moisture into his dehy-
drated mouth as possible. He looked up at her.

"What do you mean?"

"You were watching my ass when I bent over to get your
water, weren't you?"

"Couldn't help myself. You were so close. I could have
closed my eyes."

"Why didn't you?" Daisy asked.

"I've been through hell, so why shouldn't I catch just a
glimpse of heaven?"

"You call my butt *heaven*? I do declare. You *have* been
out in the sun too long."

Slocum looked at her, wondering what she was getting
at. Then she made it perfectly clear.

"My lily white behind is not my finest quality," Daisy
said primly. "Don't you agree?" She stepped back and began unbuttoning her crisply starched blouse. One button
after another popped free until he was treated to a full view
of two snowy white mounds of flesh swaying gently as she
pulled her blouse up out of the waistband of her skirt and
then shucked it off to stand bare to the waist in front of
him. She cupped both of those fine mounds, took the pink
nipples between thumb and forefinger and began squeezing down until the nubbins were hard and cherry-red.

"No," Slocum said. He saw shock spread on the half-naked woman's face.

"Wh-what do you mean?" she stammered.

"I still think that rump of yours is your best feature, though it's hard to compare, what with all that skirt hiding it."

"You want to compare the two? How?" She got over her confusion and became the same bold, wanton woman she had shown herself to be before. But Slocum knew the woman's game. She came on bold as brass but there was more than a hint of insecurity underneath it all.

"Just looking at them from across the room's no way to compare anything. In my weakened condition, my vision's a mite blurry." He felt stronger by the minute, adrenaline pumping through him.

"So how," she asked, stepping closer, "do you intend to make a decent comparison of these"—she cupped her breasts as if offering them to him on a silver platter—"with this?" Daisy turned her back to him and gave her fine posterior a twitch like a horse swatting away a buzzing fly.

"Got to do it by feel, I reckon," Slocum said. "That's the only fair way." He scooted to the edge of the bed and reached out, his hands slipping under the hem of the woman's skirt. His hands touched her silk-smooth legs. He felt her trembling like a racehorse ready to run. He wanted to join that race but held back. His hands moved up the sleek, well-muscled calves, hesitated a moment to better position himself, then began working up higher and higher. When he reached her thighs, the woman's knees gave way and she sagged back against him. Slocum kept up his exploration, his strong fingers stroking and probing, squeezing and then moving up to the vee where he found a tangled damp nest of fleecy hair. His finger slipped between the gates to her interior and moved upward into tight warmth.

This was all it took to completely rob Daisy of her

strength. She sat down suddenly, taking Slocum by surprise. His finger slid from its moist, warm berth and cupped her rounded rear end. Slocum moved his other hand around so he could stroke over the woman's ass that had so drawn him before.

"S-so?" she gasped out. "Which's better? My breasts or m-my rear?"

"Haven't checked out everything yet. Remember? I told you I had to examine everything first. By touch, because of my debilitated condition." Slocum slid his hands from beneath her, leaving her sitting on his lap looking away, as he stroked over her heaving belly. His hands worked their way up to where she still diddled with her own nips. His larger hands closed over hers and pressed down. He felt the excited hammering of her heart, even through the woman's hand still protecting her own flesh.

Slocum kissed the back of her neck and worked around to a dangling earlobe. His tongue flashed out and lightly dipped into the well of her ear before moving forward. He strained to kiss her cheek, the line of her jaw, more of her neck. Then Daisy twisted around and her mouth met his. Their lips crushed together in a passionate kiss that Slocum fed with light touches on her nipples and then a more powerful tug to draw her body into his.

He almost regretted this latter move. He had gotten excited at all he was doing and found himself painfully trapped in his jeans. His position became even more uncomfortable when Daisy half stood, widened her stance and then sat back down on his lap, her legs outside his.

"I need some help," Slocum said. He kept one arm around Daisy's waist and the other moving restlessly over her aroused nipples. "Seems both my hands are occupied. Be a real shame for me to move away from . . . this." He caught one of her taut nubs and gave it the kind of treatment she had given herself earlier. "Or this." Slocum ran his hand over the slight dome of the woman's belly and un-

der the waistband of her skirt. The button holding her skirt
on popped like a gunshot.

Neither noticed. Slocum's hand returned to the tangled
mat between her legs, slipping and sliding over the increasingly oily canyon he found there.

"I . . . I understand," Daisy got out. She gathered her
skirt up around her waist, then wiggled seductively a few
times. Slocum let her drop the unwanted garment to the
floor around her ankles. But this didn't solve his real
problem.

Daisy noticed what was troubling him most and immediately began working on the buttons holding his fly shut.
When the last button popped open, he gasped in relief. His
hardened manhood jerked upright—but it did not remain
unhindered for more than a second. Daisy's fingers
wrapped around it and began stroking.

Heat built quickly all the way into Slocum's loins. He
fought to keep from embarrassing himself like some young
buck with a woman for the first time.

But Slocum knew Daisy was more than just any woman.
She was beautiful, beguiling and intensely desirable. Her
naked hindquarters pressed seductively into his crotch, a
wiggle and twitch now and then more than enough to keep
him hard and aroused. She stroked up and down his length,
her fingers playing him like a piano. A press here, a light,
gliding touch there; Slocum knew they had both reached
the point of no return. He had to have her.

Slocum moved both hands under her, ignoring her
protests. He lifted her, rocked her forward slightly, then
positioned himself. Daisy started to say something, but her
cries turned to sobs of delight. Slocum entered her easily,
smoothly, sinking all the way to paradise.

For a moment, time stood still for him. All his senses
were inundated with her musky smell, her smooth skin, her
trembling body and fragrant hair and warmth that spread
from her body to his and consumed them both. Her soft

moans of pleasure turned into more insistent demands, even as her strong inner muscles clamped down around his hidden stalk.

"More, John, I need more. I feel like I'm just . . . hanging. Push me hard. Get me moving. Please!"

Slocum reached around her with both hands holding her in place as he began lifting off the bed and trying to stroke even deeper into her. From this position, he couldn't move. She had to do it all, and that wasn't what Slocum wanted.

It wasn't what the lovely blond woman wanted, either. She wanted a man to take command.

Slocum made a quick, powerful turn and reversed their positions. Daisy bent over the bed, supporting herself on her hands. Slocum was behind her, hanging on to keep their bodies pressed intimately together. From here he began stroking back and forth, building speed like a steam engine gathering power. His fleshy piston vanished farther and farther into her softly yielding body, every inward stroke sending a shudder of stark desire though the woman's quivering body. Slocum reached up and toyed with her dangling tits, starting at the broad bases and moving powerfully to the very tip. Once there he tweaked the nipple and then moved on. The darting, stimulating fingers kept Daisy gasping for more.

Slocum gave her more lower down. He sped up, racing in and out of her heated core until he was ready to explode. With supreme willpower he held back the fiery tide to make a few more shuddering, shivery trips in and out.

When he abandoned his manhandling of her breasts, his right hand moved to the top of the pinkly scalloped lips down low. He pressed into the tiny spire of delicate flesh. It was like pulling the trigger of a pistol. Daisy let out a loud cry of sheer release.

Her body had trembled before. Now a massive earthquake racked it. Slocum felt the powerful muscles deep inside the woman's intimate passage clamp down, squeezing him in a grip he could not escape. He had wanted to continue forever, through the night and into the next day and forever, but she robbed him of the last of his iron control. He exploded like a stick of dynamite.

His hips went wild, thrusting forward, trying to shove his hardness as deep into the woman as possible. And all too soon, he began to melt. Slocum sagged forward, following Daisy to the bed. She lay facedown on the bed, Slocum's weight pressing down on her from above.

Her rump still fit nicely into the curve of his body, but now there was a missing element. His manhood had melted like an icicle in the spring sun.

"So?" she asked.

"So?" Slocum stroked up and down her naked flanks, still enjoying the satiny feel of her flesh beneath his fingers.

"So are my tits better or my ass?"

Slocum hesitated a moment, then said, "I was too busy to come to any decision on that."

"So what are you going to do about it? You can't just let the matter rest."

"Reckon not," Slocum said, his hands still exploring the curves and planes of Daisy's fine body.

He would have been content to exhaust himself further with the woman but she surged upward tossing him into the wall.

"He's coming. Oh, no, he's coming!" Daisy flopped out of the bed and began frantically pulling up her skirt. The ripped button defeated her, so she grabbed for her blouse and slipped it on, frantically buttoning. She held her skirt together and dropped into the single chair at the small table in the center of the room, trying to look nonchalant.

"Who's coming?" Slocum asked, buttoning up his jeans. He reached for his gun belt, going for his six-gun but checked the move when Andy Stevenson opened the door.

Slocum wondered if he was going to have to shoot the young man if Andy objected to what had so obviously gone on between Slocum and Daisy.

# 5

Slocum hurriedly finished dressing, amazed that Andy Stevenson apparently didn't twig to what his sister had just been doing. He started to stand and found his legs wouldn't support him. The medicine Daisy had given him had sent blood hammering throughout his body and reinvigorated him, but being crushed by the rockfall and walking back to Victory stole away much of his strength. In spite of himself, Slocum wanted Stevenson to leave so Daisy could give him more of her special medicine.

"The gold's assayin' out to be seven or eight ounces a ton!" the young man cried. "We're going to be rich, Daisy. We're going to be richer than we ever thought."

"What gold's this?" asked Slocum from the bed. Andy noticed him for the first time.

Stevenson started to say something but the words jumbled up. He might have noticed that Slocum was here alone with Daisy but excitement overwhelmed any protest about propriety and his sister.

"From the mine we surveyed, Mr. Slocum, that's which one."

Slocum frowned. He had scouted the entire area more carefully and hadn't seen so much as a glittery fleck of gold in the stream and the Mother Lode hadn't poked out of the ground with any ore rich enough to yield eight ounces of gold for the ton. That made it more valuable than the California Gulch strike outside Leadville.

"I'm goin' to the saloon to sell more shares of stock," Stevenson said. He looked a mite sheepish, then asked, "Can I borrow some more money, Sis? Just five dollars."

"Why do you need money? Sell a share or two of your mining stock. Every share ought to be worth more than five dollars by now," Slocum said.

"I want to hang onto every last share, that's why, Mr. Slocum. That's how I get rich."

"What do you need the money for, Andy?" Daisy went to the shelf and took down a can of Clabber Girl Baking Soda, twisted off the lid and fished inside for some scrip.

"Got to pay the printer to do up more stock certificates, that's what."

"*You're* paying the printer to print the stock certificates you're selling for Aiken?" Slocum couldn't believe his ears. "Why isn't Aiken footing the bill for the printing, and why isn't he paying you to work for him?"

"He's payin' me," Stevenson said, as if lecturing a small child. "Only I'm takin' all my pay in stock. And that wasn't his idea, neither. I had to talk him into it!"

Slocum let out a long draft of air he'd been holding and tried to formulate his thoughts in a way the young man— and his sister—would understand. They were pitted against a masterful confidence man.

"Instead of spending your own money, get Aiken to pay for business expenses—*his* business expenses."

"I'm not doin' it for nuthin'," Stevenson said in the same chiding tone. "I'm gettin' *ten* dollars for the five I'm spendin'. He's repayin' me real good."

"With worthless mining stock certificates."

"John, please," Daisy said in exasperation at his failure to understand. "This is our big chance. Andy knows what that claim is worth. Mr. Aiken's been wildly successful developing gold mines. There's no reason to believe he won't be equally as successful here as he was around Denver and Colorado City." Daisy handed the five crumpled dollar bills to her brother with what Slocum thought was an air of defiance. The Stevensons, brother and sister, were bound and determined to become rich to the extent that greed blinded them.

Slocum allowed that he might be wrong about Aiken, but he didn't think so. He had seen rich men and their appetites before. A pile of money wasn't enough. They needed two piles. And if they had two, they wanted four. When four hills of money wasn't enough, they demanded four mountains. There was never an end to their greed. Aiken might be rolling in the gold from his other successful mining ventures, but nothing Slocum had seen showed the Mother Lode Mine to be anything but a mountain of drossy rock.

Slocum got to his feet and found he wobbled as he went to the table, but this might have been as much from his pleasurable time with Daisy as from the ordeal he had endured getting here.

"Sit down, John. Here's some water. You shouldn't be up and around," Daisy said, then grinned wickedly. "Might be all right if you're up but not around."

"Enough of that," he said, swatting her hand away from his crotch. He took the water and downed it. The cool liquid left a cold knot in his belly, reminding him how long it had been since he had eaten, but he was not going to take any of the woman's larder. If her brother was being paid for his work in mining stock, there'd be little enough money to spend on necessities like food.

"What are you going to do, John?"

"Don't know yet. My horse is dead, so I need to get a new mount."

"Y-you're going to ride on?"

"In a spell," he said, "but not now, not yet. I've got business here." He reached over, grabbed Daisy by the shoulders and drew her down so he could kiss her firmly on the lips. "And other reasons that have nothing to do with business," he finished.

She smiled and looked like she wanted to say something, but the words wouldn't come. The awkwardness passed when Slocum heaved himself to his feet.

"Got to get into town."

"Are you going to be back? You can stay here tonight."

"Where's your brother sleep?"

"Oh, he'll be up all night, going from one saloon to another selling the stock in the Mother Lode Mine. That's what he's done for the past couple nights. It gets mighty lonely here."

"That'd be a shame, a pretty woman like you getting all lonely."

"You think I'm pretty?"

"Quit fishing for compliments." Slocum swatted her on her pert rump, then took his leave, heading down Victory's main street. The town had grown in the short time he had been gone—or so it seemed. Activity was more frantic and men raced about, shouting and calling to one another, going into the general store like ants and emerging with a staggering amount of gear.

There was a bonanza in Victory, but it was centered in the store.

Slocum went to the livery stable and spent the better part of an hour looking over the horses before deciding on one. It took another twenty minutes to argue the drunken livery owner, Smitty, down to a reasonable price. Only then did Slocum go hunting for Andy Stevenson. He found him in the Good As Gold Drinking Emporium.

Stevenson stood on a chair at the rear of the saloon, giving his spiel as he sold shares of the mining stock. Slocum leaned against the bar, ordered a beer and tried to determine how much money changed hands. Every stock certificate could be for as little as five dollars or for a limitless amount. It all depended on the number of shares written onto the face of the bogus certificates.

"You bought yourself a few shares, Slocum?"

Slocum looked around to see Basil Aiken standing behind him, thumbs hooked into the armholes of his brocade vest.

"I need to get a few dollars ahead before I go to gambling," Slocum said.

"Gambling? You've got it all wrong, Slocum! This is a sure thing. The gold's in the ground. You and Andy saw it for yourselves." Aiken raised his voice just enough to attract the attention of the men around them. Slocum knew this was another part of the sales pitch being made.

"Can't rightly say I saw gold out there, Mr. Aiken," he said. "Folks say you have quite a nose for the metal, though."

Aiken laughed and put his thick forefinger alongside his nose and inhaled noisily.

"You might say that I'm a real bloodhound when it comes to finding gold. It's up there at the Mother Lode Mine, I tell you, Slocum. If you don't buy in now, you'll be left out."

"Won't be the first time. Doubt it'll be the last."

Aiken's bonhomie faded, and he quickly left the saloon to Stevenson's impassioned pitch at the rear. Slocum turned his attention back to the young man and marvelled at how well Andy held the crowd in thrall with his fine words. The man ought to have gone into politics. He could have won any elective office with such zeal.

"Lookee here, gents," Stevenson called, reaching into his pocket and drawing out the gold bullet Aiken had given him. "This is a symbol of what can be done—of the money that can be made by us all." He held the golden bullet aloft and let the gaslight reflect richly from it as he showed it around. "It's only a tiny bullet, not even an ounce, but it's the first of a rapid-fire flow of gold from this here mine. Buy your shares now, while there's still a few to be had."

Slocum downed his beer and pushed through the crowd when he saw trouble brewing. A drunken prospector made a grab for the bullet.

"Gimme. Lemme see it. I don't think it's real gold."

"It is real gold," Stevenson said stiffly. He closed his hand over the bullet as the prospector made a grab for it.

The prospector lurched forward and knocked Stevenson from the chair, grabbing again for the bullet. He found himself half-hoisted into the air as Slocum grabbed him by the seat of his pants and the collar of his soiled plaid flannel shirt. Slocum swung him around and gave him a bum's rush out the swinging doors into the street.

"Talk to Aiken if you want a gold bullet," Slocum said. He glared at the man who didn't appear quite so drunk now. The man sat up, stood and brushed himself off. He left without so much as a word. If he had railed and ranted, Slocum would have felt easier. Leaving the way he had warned Slocum the man had other plans—and they weren't likely to end well for Andy Stevenson.

Slocum turned back into the saloon and saw Stevenson finishing the last of the transactions. The young man wrote down the investor's name in a small ledger book before giving over a properly executed stock certificate. Slocum tried to get a look at the entries in the ledger to figure how much money Stevenson was actually collecting, but failed when Stevenson pointedly slammed the book shut to keep him from seeing.

"Thanks, Mr. Slocum. You were a real lifesaver. That drunk interfered with men who had a legitimate desire to invest." Stevenson patted his bulging coat pocket.

"What do you do with that money?"

"It goes right into Mr. Aiken's hands for deposit in his account. Or the Mother Lode Mine account, I reckon.

Right now, there're about the same thing until the actual mining starts up."

"I'll walk you to the bank."

"He doesn't use the Victory bank. Says it's like a cracker box. He wants to get all the money shipped up to Denver where the bankers know him."

"I'll stick with you a spell, then," Slocum said, uneasy at the large amount of money hinted at by the bulging coat pocket.

"There's no call for that. I can sell a few more shares in another saloon before calling it quits tonight."

Slocum looked toward the swinging doors and saw the drunk watching them closely. All trace of inebriation had gone, if he had ever been in his cups. Slocum took a couple steps in the man's direction, then stopped and turned. The crush of the crowd cut him off from Stevenson. The young man had already headed toward the back door and was leaving.

"Andy, wait!" Slocum's warning was drowned in the uproar in the Good As Gold. Two men were arm wrestling on the bar, producing cheers and grunts and loud, improbably large wagers. The surge in the crowd prevented Slocum from crossing the crowded room. He took one look and knew he could never get to the rear door in time, so he turned and ran out the swinging doors, following the path taken by the man who had tried to grab Stevenson's gold bullet.

Rounding the corner of the saloon, Slocum saw the deadly scene unwinding in front of him. The man who had pretended to be drunk earlier had stopped Stevenson, but Andy kept him at arm's length. It wasn't going to matter how far away the panhandler was. Slocum's hand flashed to his hip. He cleared leather fast and brought his Colt Navy up in a practiced movement. His thumb cocked the six-shooter, and his index finger tightened in the same movement. He hardly felt the recoil as the six-gun discharged—and robbed the man behind Stevenson of his life.

Stevenson swung around, startled. He saw the man behind him drop a drawn pistol and then slump to the ground, dead.

Slocum drew bead on the other man and started to fire. But there was no call for that. The panhandler who had stopped Stevenson hightailed it, feet pounding loudly against the ground as he ran.

"Slocum, what's going on?" Andrew Stevenson looked from the dead man to Slocum and then back. "He's dead."

"You'd be the dead one if I hadn't come along." Slocum knelt and picked up the fallen gun. He handed it to Stevenson, who took it in curiously steady hands. The young man still hadn't realized how close death had come to visiting him.

"What'm I supposed to do with this?"

"Use it to protect yourself. They were going to kill you." When Slocum saw Stevenson still didn't understand, he carefully explained it. "The drunk from the saloon wasn't so drunk."

"He tried to snatch the gold bullet Mr. Aiken had given me," said Stevenson.

"He tried to pick your pocket and take that wad of money you'd collected from selling the mining stock," Slocum said. "When that didn't work, he and his partner— the dead one on the ground at your feet—decided to dry-gulch you."

"They were going to rob me?"

"They were going to kill you, then take the money off your corpse," Slocum said harshly. He finally shook Stevenson enough to penetrate the man's naivete.

"But that's illegal!"

"With the marshal in this town so busy serving process and collecting fines for small crimes, nobody'd ever notice. And you'd be planted outside town in the potter's field."

"Oh, Mr. Aiken would never allow that," Stevenson said confidently. His hand flew to his pocket to verify that he still had the money he had collected for the mining magnate. "I better get this to Mr. Aiken right away." Stevenson stared at the six-shooter in his other hand, then tucked it into his waistband. "Thanks, Mr. Slocum. I owe you a debt of gratitude."

"I'll figure some way of collecting the debt," Slocum said, knowing there was nothing the young man could ever do to even the score.

"If you need a place to stay, ask my sister. Daisy'll find a place for you to bed down."

"Thanks," Slocum said dryly.

"I . . . I better get a move on. Thanks again." Stevenson edged around the fallen robber and then almost ran. Slocum watched him go. His mind raced. He could return to Daisy's shack and collect a bit of the debt the Stevenson family owed him—or he could add to that debt.

Slocum got ready to ride out of town at dawn.

# 6

Slocum stared at the mountains ahead as he rode along the railroad tracks of the narrow-gauge line giving lifeblood to Victory. He was three days out and might have ridden the train to Denver, but he preferred the feel of the saddle under him, and if nothing else, to get the sense of the new horse. He was sorry to see the gelding crushed under the rockfall, but the roan responded well to his commands, as if reading his mind. Which turned out to be good since he was thinking hard about Basil Aiken and the Mother Lode Mine and how Stevenson was being duped into selling worthless stock certificates.

And more than a bit of his thought fleetingly touched on Daisy Stevenson. The spark between them was undeniable. The instant she had set eyes on him, she had become bolder and more sure of herself. The slight stutter when she showed indecision told him how much he had affected her. She was a lovely woman, and the feeling was mutual.

But she was as caught up in the overwhelming greed Aiken generated as her brother. Slocum could talk till he was blue in the face and not convince her there was no gold in the claim Andy had staked out. What proof he might find backtracking to Aiken's other claims remained to be seen, but Slocum felt he had to try. He hated to see anyone so thoroughly bilked by a confidence man, and his gut told him Aiken was dealing off the bottom of the deck with Andy Stevenson asking for new cards all on his own.

All those thoughts occupied him so Slocum was glad for the break when the horse shied suddenly.

"Whoa, what's wrong?" Slocum patted the roan's neck, tipped his head to one side and listened hard. He thought the horse had heard an approaching train, but he heard and saw nothing. If an engine steamed toward him along the mountain-laid rails, the plume of smoke ought to be visible since the tracks stretched out in a fairly straight line for a mile or more before rising steadily into a higher stretch of the Rockies.

He turned slowly in the saddle until a whiff of burning piñon wrinkled his nose. Campfire. Almost simultaneously he heard nickering horses. At least two men, probably more. Then came a resounding blast that shook the ground and spooked his horse.

Slocum turned his horse's face in the direction of the echo from the explosion and rode slowly into the hills a mile or so away from the railroad tracks. Every sense strained to detect the men responsible for the blast since he had no idea what he was getting himself into. But it might have been an accidental blast with injured miners needing help.

In this part of Colorado it could be something more.

Slocum drew rein at the top of a low ridge looking down into a broad valley. The grassland looked perfect for cattle or a herd of horses, but no one had claimed the verdant meadow for that purpose. Off to one side, halfway up the slope, billowed a brown cloud betraying the location where the blast had ripped part of the guts from the mountain.

Pulling field glasses from his saddlebags, Slocum studied the area carefully. He saw two men staggering around downslope from the blast. That they hadn't been safely out of the way meant either they were inept or that the blast had gone off prematurely. Either way hinted they might need Slocum's help. He heaved a sigh and rode deliberately in the direction of the mine.

Halfway there he saw a crudely lettered sign: HEAVENS ABOVE. Slocum hoped the explosion hadn't sent any of the miners to the Promised Land. This part of the Rockies wasn't likely to give up gold as much as lead or even coal.

"Hello!" Slocum called when he got close enough. The air was still filled with dust, though much of it had already settled. A more acrid odor told how much Giant Blasting Powder the miners had used—Slocum was no expert but guessed they had used three or four times the amount needed to open a decent hole in the ground.

"Who're you?"

"You need help? I was riding past and heard the explosion."

"Git on outta here," growled a grizzled miner. He staggered down the slope, clutching a pickax in his hands. His face was almost black with soot and his tough canvas clothing had been torn by the hot gases rushing from the mouth of the mine. If he had been inside, he would have been dead.

"Hold on, Rip, hold yer danged horses," called another, flopped on the ground under a stunted scrub oak tree. "I got me a busted leg. You don't know squat 'bout fixin' it, and I ain't gonna lop it off 'cuz you're so dumb."

The man was obviously in a bad way; his leg bent at a peculiar angle above the knee showing the severity of his injury.

"What's it going to be?" Slocum called to the one still brandishing the pickax, waving it around menacingly. "I've set a leg or two in my day, but then I've hacked off a leg or two, as well, during the war. Don't much like doing any doctoring, but I can."

"Rip, you ignoramus, let the gent get down and see what he kin do for my leg."

Rip lowered his pick, then tossed it aside, glowering at Slocum.

"All right, you go have a look-see at my partner. But you kill him and I swear, you're buzzard bait!"

"You make it real attractive to keep on riding," Slocum said.

"Rip!"

Rip looked over his shoulder at his partner and slumped. He turned his burned, filthy face up at Slocum and said, "All right. Do what you kin. He's busted up bad. I know that. But don't let him die. All right?"

"I'll see what can be done," Slocum said, dismounting. He tethered his roan so it could munch at the juicy meadow grass and then advanced slowly, giving Rip time to adjust to the presence of another human being. Miners were solitary creatures and didn't take kindly to other men intruding on their private domains.

"You surely did bung yourself up," Slocum said. Jagged white bone showed through the miner's pants leg. "What happened?"

"We got fed up and wanted to close our mine, so we set off all the black powder we had. Reckon the fuse was shorter 'n we planned."

Slocum went to draw his knife from its sheath in his right boot top and cut away the cloth but came up empty-handed. He had given the knife to the Ute. He knew there was nothing to do but use his hands. He probed gently to get a feel for the extent of the miner's wound.

"You got a name?" Slocum asked.

"Gladstone, but my friends call me Glad."

"Reckon I'd better call you Gladstone, then, because you're not going to think of me as your friend." To Rip, Slocum called, "Bring me all the whiskey you've got."

"We was savin' it," Rip said.

"This is what you were saving it for," said Slocum. With

a steel edge to his voice, he commanded, "Bring it all. Every last drop."

"You think you kin save the leg?"

"Maybe so," said Slocum. "But no matter what, they're going to call you Gimpy Gladstone afterward."

"Just so's I kin kick the bastards in the ass now 'n then."

Slocum looked around and found some sturdy saplings and hacked them down using Rip's abandoned pickax. While he waited for Rip to return with the miners' hootch, he measured the saplings and cut them for the proper length to act as splints. By the time he had torn away Gladstone's pants leg and cut the material into strips, Rip staggered back with two bottles of cheap rotgut.

"Here. Don't go drinkin' none. It's ours," Rip said sullenly.

"Start drinking," Slocum said, thrusting one bottle in Gladstone's direction. "As much as you can take without puking up your guts."

"He's got a hollow leg," declared Rip. The miner clamped his mouth shut when he realized what that might mean if Slocum couldn't save the leg.

Slocum took the other bottle, having to pry it loose from Rip's fingers, pulled the cork and began pouring it all over the protruding end of the bone. It fizzed a little, and Slocum missed with another few drops when Gladstone jerked in response.

"That hurts worse 'n 'bout anything I ever felt," he said.

"Wait a few minutes," Slocum said, sitting back on his haunches. The whiskey Gladstone guzzled had to take some of the edge off the pain, but it wouldn't be anywhere near enough. To Rip he said, "You strong enough to hold him or you want to tie him down so he doesn't thrash around too much?"

"Tie him down?" Rip sounded like he was the one in shock.

"He'll probably pass out, but if he doesn't, we ought to be prepared. And you need to build a small fire."

"Why?"

"So I can heat the blade of that knife you've got sheathed at your side. Some of the flesh around the wound's got to be cut away, then I have to cauterize it after I get the bone back into position."

"Do it, Rip. Do it." Gladstone sounded dreamy now, the liquor taking its hold on his senses. Slocum poked again with the tip of Rip's reluctantly surrendered knife and the miner didn't respond. Things were going well. So far.

Slocum watched Rip do the small chores he had set for him as much to keep him busy and out of the way as because he needed the fire or ropes to hold Gladstone down. But the time finally came for him to do what he could.

"You hold on as hard as you can. It's real important," Slocum said. "Grab him under the arms. If I say pull, you pull hard. Got that?"

"He's almost passed out," Rip said uncertainly.

"Good."

When the miner had his partner in a secure grip and had braced his own feet, Slocum took the injured leg and began applying a firm, steady pressure. Gladstone let out a shriek of pure agony before he passed out. Slocum kept pulling. He felt movement within the leg as the bone slid back into place, but he had to pull with all his might before he felt the snap of the ends of the fracture clicking back together. Even then Slocum wasn't sure how good the match was. The bone had been on the ragged side, but he knew better than to go poking around inside the man's leg. Gladstone had been lucky no arteries had been severed. He would have bled to death in a matter of minutes.

"Enough," Slocum said to Rip. He began pressing the hot knife blade to the flesh to burn it, to seal it against further damage. Then he secured the saplings around Gladstone's leg to hold it immobile. A half hour later, Slocum sat down and wiped sweat from his forehead.

"Will he be . . . will he die?"

"Can't say, but I don't think so. It's going to take a month or two for him to walk on that leg, though."

"I kin nurse him."

"Let's get him to your cabin," Slocum said. With Rip fussing like a mother hen, they picked up the injured miner and got him to the ramshackle hut perched on the side of the mountain.

"I kin watch over him. We got food 'nuff for that, then we kin hightail it 'fore winter hits too hard."

Slocum looked around the cabin and saw how they had sealed the chinks in the log walls. Most miners used mud. They had crammed paper into the holes. Slocum pried one free and stared at it with a sinking feeling in his belly.

"That there's 'bout all the stock cer-tiffy-kit's good fer," Rip said. "That son of a bitch done sold us a ton of worthless mining stock. He knowed this was a bad claim, but he sold it to us. If I ever git my hands on him—"

"Would the gent's name be Basil Aiken, by any chance?"

"Him's the one!" roared Rip. "He stole from us as sure as if he upped and shoved a gun under our noses. He sold us this empty hole. Thass why we blowed it up. It's not got a flake of gold in it."

"There are a lot of stock certificates," Slocum said.

"We bought into other mines. Surefire, he said. They was all worthless, too. He done a couple dozen of us out of our money, good men and true all the way to Denver. If I ever git my hands on him . . ."

"You be willing to come to Victory and tell some friends about what Aiken did?"

"You said Glad's not gonna move fer a month or two."

"I said that," Slocum replied. His heart sank. He had

proof that Aiken was racing across Colorado selling bogus stock certificates to unsuspecting men. He had branched out now, letting Andrew Stevenson do his dirty work for him. All Aiken had to do was sit back, hike his feet to a desktop and smoke a cigar while the money flowed in. Worse, when the people around Victory figured out how they had been bamboozled, they'd blame Stevenson. Aiken could get away before the law ever got to him—or a lynch mob found a suitable tree limb.

"Why'd you have to burn him like that?" Rip peered at the blackened section of skin where Slocum had cauterized it with the heated knife.

"Keeps down the chance of getting a fever. Not sure why, but I've seen it work. You watch him close. If he gets a fever, pour water over him and make him as comfortable as you can."

"Thanks, mister. I'd give you a gold nugget—if there'd been anything but granite in this here mine." Rip looked at his partner. "I'd offer some food, too, but I ain't got much to spare, not if Glad here's gonna be laid up fer a couple months."

"Any other miners around here give Aiken their money? I'd like to talk to them, maybe get them to come back to Victory with me."

"You a lawman? You don't look like one."

"Just somebody who doesn't like to see folks like you lose money to a crook."

"I'd go with you, if I could. Glad, too. We're mad as hell 'bout what that son of a bitch done. But I don't know where there's anybody else. Most of 'em quit long 'fore we did. Don't know if we were stupid or not. Thought we was jist more dedicated to gittin' rich."

"Aiken made a fortune with legit mines."

"That's what gulled us. We checked on him that much. He made millions off real gold strikes. He has a nose for gold, so ever'one said. I'd kill him, I would, him and his damn nose."

Slocum stuffed a few of the stock certificates into his pocket, then slipped from the cabin. He had done what he could, maybe saved Gladstone's life, maybe just postponed the inevitable. He would never know, but he could hope.

Slocum mounted his horse and headed back toward Victory. He might be able to save Andy—and Daisy—some embarrassment and a whole lot of money. Depending on how the people of Victory acted when they found how worthless the mining stock was that Stevenson was selling them, Slocum might even save the young man's life.

# 7

Slocum rode toward gunfire. He reached over and pulled the leather thong off the hammer of his Colt Navy, then drew it and checked to be sure it was ready for action. Normally he rode with the hammer resting on an empty chamber, so he had five shots. He quickly decided not to take time to load the sixth because the gunfire from the direction of Victory increased. It sounded as if a small war had broken out.

When he caught the acrid scent of gunpowder on the wind—and even saw white clouds of gun smoke rising—he knew there was a mighty big fight in progress.

Slocum spurred his roan forward at a trot, then slowed when he reached the edge of town. He expected to see the buildings falling down, their walls shot full of holes. Instead, cheering crowds filled the streets. Men danced arm-in-arm and the few women he saw all stood on the boardwalks under canopies, laughing and talking. A new round of gunshots echoed along the street but no one took notice.

When an earthshaking explosion went off, the dancing stopped, but only for a moment.

"What's going on?" Slocum called to a man too drunk

to stand up. The miner clung to a hitching post and an empty whiskey bottle with equal determination. The man turned bloodshot eyes toward Slocum, belched and then laughed.

"Hell 'n damnation, man, where you been? They found it. They found it!"

The miner hiccuped, then bent forward and spun around the hitching rail to land flat on his back. He stared up at the blue Colorado sky. Slocum saw he wasn't likely to get any information from the drunken miner. He rode forward toward the knot of men still dancing.

"What's the celebration about?" Slocum shouted. A half dozen men turned and bellowed back.

"Gold! They done found gold! We're all gonna be rich!"

A few of the men pulled out stock certificates in the Mother Lode Mine and waved them around. They began chanting "Rich, rich, rich" and snaked off through the middle of town.

Slocum dismounted and led his horse to the livery stables, put it into a stall and made sure it had a bag of grain for its loyal service. The stable hand could tend the horse later. Right now, Slocum wanted to find out what was going on. The best one to ask was Daisy Stevenson.

The merrymaking was in full swing, aided and abetted by several saloons bringing out barrels of whiskey for the townspeople. Men came over and dipped tin cups of the potent rotgut and downed it before sampling another and being shoved out of the way by other thirsty celebrants. Slocum edged along the crowd, jostled by the singing, laughing men as he went toward a spot where a group of women stood apart. He thought he saw Daisy there.

"Oh, John, you're back! Where'd you go? Oh, this is so wonderful!" Daisy launched herself from the boardwalk. Slocum caught her easily and spun her about before setting her down on the ground. She looked up at him, then impulsively kissed him full on the lips.

"We're in public," he started.

"Oh, bother!" she cried. "Everyone's celebrating. Victory is going to be put on the map with the discovery. It's rich, John, it's richer than even Mr. Aiken thought it would be. The first load of ore's out of the mine and it's fabulous! And he knows. He's an expert." She clung to him tightly, making Slocum a bit embarrassed at such a public display. But Daisy was right. No one took notice. They were too busy with their own particular ways of celebration.

"What happened?" he asked.

"Gold, John, the Mother Lode Mine is just that—the mother lode! That means Andy and I are rich! We own thousands of shares of stock in the mine!"

Slocum didn't bother pointing out that about everyone else in Victory did, too. Split so many ways, even the richest gold mine ever found wouldn't make any single investor rich. Or maybe it would make one richer.

Basil Aiken.

Slocum heaved a deep sigh. He might have it all wrong. The two miners, Gladstone and Rip, might have been sour because they had not found gold at all and Aiken had. Victory might be just that, a triumph of Aiken's skill in sniffing out gold like a bloodhound follows a coon. As Daisy moved against him, Slocum felt the tattered stock certificates he had taken from the miners' shack crumple a bit more in his pocket.

"You should have bought shares of the mine, John. You'd be rich, too."

"If the stock's worth more—"

"It is, now that gold's been found!"

"Why not sell a few shares and get your stake back?"

"What's wrong with you?" Daisy shoved away from him and glared. "You might not want to be rich, but Andy and I certainly do! We're buying more stock, not selling what we have. It's a sure thing, John. *A sure thing!*"

Before Slocum could say a word, a cheer went up, and

he and Daisy were carried along with the crowd to the end of town where Aiken had erected his stage. It was hung with fresh red, white and blue bunting. Standing at the edge, thumbs tucked under the armholes of his vest, Basil Aiken waited for the cheers to die down before he spoke. He grinned ear to ear, the biggest shit-eating grin Slocum had ever seen. And why not? He was rich and had made the entire town of Victory rich.

"Ladies and gents, you don't want to hear me do any talking," Aiken said. "You want to hear it firsthand from the fellow who brought in the gold. I hired Clyde Touhy, an experienced, expert miner of the first water, to come in from Denver and prove the claim. It took him less than a day to find the vein running throughout the claim and going deep into the mountain. The Mother Lode Mine is going to be just that—a mother lode for us all!"

A new cry of joy went up, almost deafening Slocum. He looked out of the corner of his eye and saw Daisy cheering as wildly as any of the men. Everyone in town was caught up in the fever of gold.

The short, graying miner shuffled forward. He let Aiken put his arm around his shoulder, as if they were old friends. Then he grinned to match his employer, showing a missing tooth in front.

"See this?" Touhy said, pointing to the gap in his teeth. "I ain't leavin' it that way. No, siree. I'm havin' yer town dentist fix me up with a gold tooth. A gold tooth made from the first nugget I pulled from the Mother Lode Mine!" He held up a chunk of gold large enough to catch the sunlight and cast its golden reflection over the crowd like some holy benediction.

"Is there a dentist in Victory?" called Aiken from just behind the miner. "Anywhere?"

"I pass for one," spoke up a man near the front of the crowd.

"You pass out at the sight of blood, that's what you do, Lester!" joked someone else in the crowd.

"I can make a tooth," Lester insisted. "I done it before."

"Here you go," Touhy said, tossing the nugget down. "You make me the dangedest, best front tooth ever made. And keep the rest of the gold for your fee!"

A new cheer went up—and Slocum found himself on edge. He had the feeling he watched a carefully planned sideshow. Instead of snake oil being sold to the crowd, it was gold fever.

"We can all get gold teeth," someone at the edge of the crowd declared. Slocum tried to see who it was but the man moved away quickly, heading for the back of the crowd.

"You will be able to hire someone to chew your food for you, you're all going to be so rich," said Aiken, laughing. He slapped Touhy on the back. "Go on, my good man. Tell them everything!"

"I went to the spot surveyed and claimed by Mr. Aiken's able assistant, Andrew Stevenson—"

Daisy let out a cheer that was picked up by others nearby.

"I went to where Andy Stevenson said and began rooting around. Took me purt-near all day to begin digging into the side of the hill and pokin' up was the nugget I just tossed down to Lester there."

A new cheer went up. Slocum turned and saw the man at the back of the crowd who had started the cry moving to the far side of the gathering. He kept his eyes on him and watched as he initiated more than one cheer that was anything but spontaneous. Slocum's attention strayed from the golden tales spun by Clyde Touhy as he watched Aiken. For a man who had just made a new fortune, Aiken looked less excited as he did conniving.

Touhy finished with an introduction of Andy Stevenson, who said, "You're not too late, folks. We still got shares in the Mother Lode Mine, but they're pricier now. Lots pricier, but you can still get on the bandwagon. Don't shove, come on up, Mr. Aiken and me'll sell you all the shares you want."

Stevenson had said his boss would help sell, but it was Touhy who took over the chore. Aiken drifted to the rear of the stage, then dropped down behind. Slocum pushed his way through the crowd to catch a glimpse of Aiken, the man who had prompted the crowd with his cheers and another hard case talking in low tones. Aiken pointed toward the mountains where the Mother Lode Mine lay, then reached into his vest pocket and pulled out something Slocum couldn't see. He repeated this, taking small objects from his coat pocket and giving them to the two men.

Aiken slapped both on the shoulder and came toward Slocum. Slocum ducked back into the Good As Gold Saloon and let the mining magnate pass by, whistling "My Darling Clementine" as he went. He didn't appear to have a care in the world, but why should he? Slocum stepped back out and looked at the man's broad back as he disappeared down the street. Following him wouldn't get Slocum any more information than he already had.

He went to the stage and looked for the pair of men Aiken had spoken to. Slocum's curiosity made him wonder what the mining magnate had fished out of his pocket and handed to the men. Above his head on stage, Stevenson and Touhy hawked shares in the mine. Slocum looked around the side and saw Daisy helping keep the line waiting to purchase more shares in the mine all nice and orderly. She was as caught up in the selling as her brother.

Slocum went to the stables and made sure his roan had water before saddling up again and riding out, to the horse's great protests. It had already been a long day and was about to get longer. Instinct guiding him now, Slocum headed for the far side of Victory and the trail leading toward the Mother Lode Mine. He wasn't too surprised to see fresh tracks leading away.

The road had been well enough travelled that he could not determine if a single horse or two had come this way, but he reckoned it was two. Aiken's two henchmen.

As the sun dipped behind the mountains ahead, Slocum saw how the tracks separated enough to show distinct hoof-prints. Two riders. Both heading in the same direction—for the mine.

Slocum touched the worthless mining certificates in his pocket, then rode on with determination. His head told him one thing but his gut said another. Aiken had been success-ful finding precious metal before. Gladstone and Rip's fail-ure meant nothing. No one, not even a successful miner like Aiken, scored every time. They might have been un-fortunate amid a sea of successes.

That was what Slocum's head told him. There was more than a tad of doubt. But his instincts screamed that Aiken was a fraud out to bilk the people of Victory—and the Stevensons—of a whale of a lot of money.

He rode steadily through the night, then slower as he neared the claim just before sunup. When he heard the two men talking in level tones ahead, he dismounted, stashed his horse in a stand of pines and advanced on foot. The rocky ground sloped away toward the hilly area where he had run afoul of the avalanche that had almost robbed him of his life.

Slocum's hand flashed to his six-shooter when he heard the first gunshot. Then came the two men's voices drifting on the dawn. They weren't in the least upset. This sent Slocum moving forward as silent as any Navajo scout to the edge of the claim. He knelt behind the stone cairn An-drew Stevenson had erected to mark the boundary of the mine.

Another gunshot. Slocum identified the deep-throated bellow as a shotgun. In the dim light he moved closer to where the men stood just inside a depression in the side of the hill. Clyde Touhy had worked like a mole burrowing into the rocky mountainside. Again a touch of doubt worried away at Slocum. Touhy might have dug in far enough to unearth the vein of ore that produced his flashy nugget. If the two men in the mouth of the mine spotted him, they might take him for a high-grader and open fire. Slocum knew they had a shotgun in addition to their sidearms.

Another roar filled the still morning air. This time laughter accompanied it. The men stepped from the mine, took off their hats and waved them about to dispel the cloud of gunpowder that filled the mouth of the shallow mine.

"That oughta do it. Let's go tell Aiken."

"When's he bringin' them rubes out here?"

"Tomorrow, later, what's the difference?"

"I want to get paid," protested the second man, resting the shotgun over his shoulder like a soldier getting ready to go on parade. "This here's dangerous work."

"Beats shootin' people when we rob 'em," said the first, laughing even harder. Together the men mounted their horses and rode back in the direction of Victory.

Slocum waited a few minutes to be certain they were well on the trail, then made his way to the mouth of the mine. Touhy had chewed away a good six feet of rock and had crudely shored it. From the look, he had blasted expertly to get this far so fast.

A deep sniff convinced Slocum the two men had fired the shotgun inside the shallow mine. He fumbled in his pocket and drew out the tin with several lucifers. He struck one, held it high and looked at the walls and roof of the mine. Bright golden smears reflected richly.

He stooped and held the match just a few inches above the floor, reached out and picked up a spent shotgun shell.

"Now that's downright careless," Slocum said to himself. He peered into the cardboard cylinder and saw the same golden smears. Aiken had loaded the shotgun shell with gold dust and sent his henchmen to the Mother Lode Mine to salt it.

Slocum fished a smoke from his pocket, used the dying flame of the lucifer to light it, then sat with his back against the salted mine wall and smoked as he thought. This time both head and heart told him the same thing.

# 8

John Slocum had no idea how to convince Daisy and her brother to stop selling the bogus mining stock certificates and begin cashing in to get back what they were due. As far as anyone in Victory was concerned, the Mother Lode Mine was their gatepost on the road to wealth. Aiken helped this notion along with his largesse, giving away huge sums of money and spending lavishly, all the while telling the people they would be rich enough to spend money like water someday, too.

"You don't understand the principle of the pyramid, John," Daisy said patiently, as if talking to the village idiot. "We've built a fine base. Now we need to continue stacking more on top. The cheap stock will make us the most money but we use it as a lever to get more shares, although they cost more."

"It's a good idea in any poker game you're winning to take enough chips off the table to equal your stake. That way you're playing with the house's money." He saw his analogy was as alien to her as hers was to him.

"But we're getting rich!"

"You're likely to watch a noose dropped over your brother's head," Slocum said, "when the good citizens of

Victory find they've been swindled, they'll strike out. When that happens I suspect Aiken will be long gone, leaving Andy holding the bag."

"Oh, John. I don't know what I'm going to do with you." Daisy grinned her wicked grin and batted her long eyelashes. "I know what I'd like to do, though. And I would, except I have a business appointment."

"What business?" Slocum wasn't sure he wanted to find out.

"I've gone to work for Mr. Aiken as an associate."

"You're selling stock, too. That'll mean you and your brother are likely to swing together from some sturdy tree limb."

"I can never tell when you're joking," she said, shaking her head. "No, Mr. Aiken didn't think the investors would be as likely to trust a woman with their money, but he is."

"I don't understand."

Daisy leaned closer, looked around and then whispered, "I'm a courier and will be taking a special parcel to Denver for him."

"When?"

"Well, I wasn't supposed to say anything to anyone since this is a secret mission, but I've already got a ticket on the next train to Denver. He's entrusting me with a very important package."

"What is it?"

"I don't know, and if he had wanted me to know, Mr. Aiken would have told me. All I need to know is where to deliver it." Daisy scowled prettily, then added, "I'm not sure I ought to have told you even this much. You won't tell anyone else, will you, John?"

Slocum wasn't sure anyone in Victory would care. They were too embroiled in their wild celebration of gold being discovered in a salted mine. His hand drifted to the coat pocket where he had the spent shotgun shell and considered again the chance Daisy might believe that Aiken was running a gigantic swindle on the entire town. His hand slipped from the shell outlined in the cloth. It would take more than this, more than Rip and Gladstone's worthless stock certificates, to prove to her everything wasn't exactly as Aiken said.

Even if she witnessed his two henchmen salting the claim, that might not be enough since she didn't know or understand the first thing about mining gold. This made the scam all the more distasteful for Slocum. People driven by greed and ignorance were always easy victims.

"I won't breathe a word to a soul," he said.

"I knew I could count on you. This is an important mission, and I'm being rewarded handsomely for it."

"In gold dust?"

"Why, in stock! That's better than gold—right now. I've got to go tend to my chores." Daisy looked around, saw no one looking in their direction and gave Slocum a quick peck on the lips. She drew back, heaved a sigh that made her breasts rise and fall delightfully, then said, "I wish we had time." With that, she turned and hurried off, holding her skirts up to keep the hem from dragging in the dust.

Slocum settled into a chair and watched the rush around him. Supplies poured into Victory, making a fortune for the merchants—those that weren't beholden to Aiken. Slocum guessed most of them were splitting their profits with the mining magnate, increasing Aiken's fortune daily, without having to sell any of the bogus stock certificates. Down the street, the town marshal had a few prisoners out filling in potholes, as befitted a town about to explode at the seams when news of the gold strike reached the rest of the territory. The marshal even had two miscreants loading garbage into a wagon and another flinging the dead bodies of dogs and other small animals into a pile to be removed later. Victory might end up the cleanest town west of the Mississippi thanks to Aiken and his scheming.

It was too great a price to pay for what they got.

Slocum fumbled in his shirt pocket and pulled out the wad of greenbacks riding there. He counted through them twice and did some calculations. A slow smile came to his lips. He got up and went to the livery stables to make certain he could keep his horse and gear here for the week or so he intended to be gone—on the train to Denver. Daisy didn't know it but she was going to have a shadow following her, protecting her. Something about her story didn't ring true to Slocum. Since he believed the worst of Aiken already, adding a bit of mayhem intended to harm a lovely blond lady wasn't out of the question.

From the stables Slocum went to the train depot and bought a round-trip ticket and then found himself a place in the shade to wait and think. After twenty minutes he grew restive but remained where he was when the train chuffed into the station. As the crew worked to load more wood into the tender and water for the boiler, the conductor punched tickets for the boarding passengers.

Slocum saw Daisy primly hand her ticket to the conductor, who tipped his hat politely and motioned her to the first-class passenger car adjoining the sleeper. She clutched two pieces of luggage, one a full-sized suitcase and the other a small case. She refused the conductor's help with either. Slocum had purchased only a ticket, not one entitling him to a bunk along the way, but he didn't worry on this score. He could sleep standing up, if need be. What he didn't want was for Daisy to spot him. There would be questions he didn't want to answer, and the recriminations on her part might be extreme.

Settling onto a hard seat in the passenger car immediately behind the tender, Slocum tilted his hat down and dozed off until the train whistle let out an ear-splitting screech, metal grated on metal, and the train began slowly pulling out of the station. After a few minutes of rattling along the narrow-gauge tracks, Slocum fell into the rhythm of the train and slipped off to sleep again. The following midday the train pulled into the Denver depot.

Slocum was well rested and exited before Daisy would have had time to gather her belongings and stuff them into the two cases she carried. He flopped onto a bench and drew down his hat so he could peer out just under the brim. She might recognize him yet but when the lovely blonde exited, she was completely intent on managing her two cases and getting about her business.

He jumped to his feet to follow, then froze. Getting off the train from the car immediately behind the one where Slocum had ridden was one of the men who had salted the Mother Lode Mine. Slocum waited to see if his partner would also get off but the man appeared to be alone—and trailing Daisy.

Slocum hurried forward but by now the crowd had surged onto the platform, wanting to board the train. These passengers mingled with those trying to get off, causing a crush that Slocum wasn't able to force through. By the time he reached the broad street in front of the railroad depot, both Daisy and her tracker were gone.

Asking after the woman would do no good. The hangers-on would lie to him, even if he paid them for the information. Especially if he did, because they would see future payoffs for added details. He turned in a full circle, then went to the side of the main depot and clambered up a drainpipe. This drew curious stares, but no one tried to stop him. When he got to the roof, he swung around and used this vantage to look up and down the street. One direction led out into the countryside. Behind him lay the train yards and the only promising direction was along the street leading down the middle of Denver. Slocum had spent many a night in the saloons in Larimer Square, but that wasn't Daisy's most likely destination.

Shielding his eyes, he peered around and finally saw her

walking quickly almost a quarter mile off. He was lucky that she hadn't hired one of the carriages lined up at the railroad station. He guessed that Basil Aiken hadn't given her enough money for that—and the hacks wouldn't take Mother Lode Mine stock certificates as payment. Letting go of his grip, Slocum slid back to the ground, hit hard and was off at a trot following Daisy. He had not spotted Aiken's crony, but he had to be somewhere between Slocum and Daisy Stevenson.

As Slocum made his way through the crowd and caught sight of the woman's hat bouncing up and down, occasionally visible through the throng, he slowed and began looking for Aiken's henchman. He might learn more taking the man aside and asking some pointed questions than he ever could following Daisy. But as alert as Slocum was, he failed to spot the man. Rather than lose Daisy in the rush, Slocum closed the distance between them until he was only a dozen paces back.

She had lived in Denver and knew the streets better than he did. She turned this way and that, getting away from the hordes of people. Slocum kept up—barely—but nowhere did he catch sight of the other man until Daisy stopped in front of a bank on Cherry Creek Street. Her rapid pace from the railroad station had taken its toll on her stamina, and she put down the large suitcase she carried, holding the smaller one close to her body, then began fishing around inside it.

The man from the train rounded the corner as Daisy dug about inside the small case. He hesitated and Slocum caught a look of surprise on the man's face. Slocum had no time to figure out what had startled the man because he shrugged, straightened his arms and walked briskly in Daisy's direction. Slocum saw the flash of a knife in the noonday sun as he advanced on Daisy, the weapon held down close to his side but ready for a swift upward killing thrust.

Slocum's hand went to his six-gun but he didn't have a good shot, not with people crossing back and forth in front of him.

"Daisy!" he shouted. "Look out! Go into the bank!"

Daisy Stevenson stopped digging in her small case and looked around, confused.

"He's trying to rob you! Run, Daisy, run!"

Slocum shoved his way through the people, using his pistol barrel to help them move faster than they would have without such a prod. When he got closer he levelled the gun and shouted, "Drop the knife!"

Aiken's henchman swung around. His arm came back and then snapped forward in a smooth, practiced movement. The knife cartwheeled through the air for Slocum. Slocum fired but missed. The knife grazed his arm, leaving behind a bloody scratch that looked worse than it felt. Clattering to the ground, the knife lay wet with Slocum's blood and the lost promise of a death.

Slocum fired but missed again. The bullet ricocheted off the bank's stone wall beside the man's head and sent chips flying everywhere. These were more effective driving people away than the actual bullets.

"John?"

"Stay down!" Slocum shouted at the confused blond woman. He raced to the alley beside the bank where the man had disappeared. He was ready to fire, but he had no target. The man had vanished like smoke on the wind. Disgusted, he rammed his six-shooter back into his holster and returned to Daisy.

"You're hurt," she said, reaching out to touch the slashed sleeve, now sticky with blood.

"I'll be all right," he said. "He didn't hurt you."

"Who's that? What are you talking about? And why are you here in Denver?"

"Come on inside. You were coming here, weren't you?"

"Why, yes, this is where Mr. Aiken told me to deliver

the suitcase." To Slocum's surprise, she picked up the large suitcase and held it out rather than the smaller grip.

"These are my spare clothes," she said, seeing him staring at the small case.

"What's in the suitcase?"

"I don't know. It's a secret. I have a letter—" She set down the cases and pulled a sealed envelope from her handbag. "I don't know what instructions are here, either. If Mr. Aiken had wanted me to know, he would have told me."

"Come along," Slocum said, taking her elbow and leading her to the alley where Aiken's henchman had gone. A quick glance assured Slocum they were alone, or as alone as they could be in a big town like Denver. He took the letter from her and considered it.

"You can't read it. It's for someone inside."

"The man who tried to knife you works for Aiken. I saw them talking in Victory."

"That does not prove he works for Mr. Aiken," she pointed out. "Many people talk to him. He is a wealthy man, after all, with many business connections."

Slocum fingered the letter and knew the contents were important proof, but Daisy gave him no chance to open the envelope and read the letter. She snatched it away, stamped her foot and waggled her finger at him.

"You are too suspicious, John. Really. I am working. Let me do my job."

"I'll go with you, to see you arrive safely."

"It's only a few feet," Daisy argued but the small smile on her lips told Slocum she was appreciative of the offer. They entered the bank and looked around.

"There," she said. "There's Mr. Skinner."

Slocum saw a rail-thin man with a walrus mustache at a desk. Daisy had failed to mention that Cornelius Skinner was the bank president. They went over and Daisy introduced herself.

"And you, sir?" asked the bank president in a surprisingly deep voice.

"I'm along to make sure this arrives," Slocum said, lifting the suitcase to the desktop. It was heavier than he expected, making him wonder anew what was inside. "You want to check the contents and give us a receipt for it?" Slocum hoped to get a glimpse into the case.

Daisy handed the letter to Skinner who opened and read it carefully. He took eyeglasses from his desk drawer, cleaned the lenses and put them on and read the letter a second time, as if he might have missed something.

"Very well," Skinner said. "I'll see that the contents are properly credited to the new account."

"Where's it all going?" Slocum asked.

"There's no call for you to ask that, John. It's none of your business. It's none of *our* business." Daisy scowled at him.

"You go with him and count the money in the suitcase," Slocum said. Daisy's eyebrows rose in surprise and she mouthed "Money?" so that only he saw.

"That will be acceptable, miss. Please come with me to the counting room."

Slocum had made a guess as to the contents and scored a bull's-eye. He opened the gate in the low railing for Daisy to accompany the bank president into the counting room and then looked around. The bank lobby was deserted, tellers looking bored and the lone guard sitting in a chair by the front door, trying not to nod off. Slocum went to him.

"Am I ever glad to deliver that," Slocum said, making a big show of wiping sweat from his forehead.

"What's it?" asked the guard, blinking sleepily.

"Another pile of money from Basil Aiken."

"'Bout time, too," the guard said. "We was all bettin' how long it'd take 'fore he delivered. His wife's gettin' real antsy, and when she gets riled, there's always hell to pay."

"Spends money fast?" suggested Slocum. The guard laughed.

"He's damn near broke all the time keepin' her in fancy jewels and in that big house on North Hill. Jist payin' the servants for a week costs more 'n I make in a year. Or so I hear."

"But Aiken's rich," Slocum said.

"Ain't no man rich enough to keep a spendthrift wife *and* a herd of fillies like him. Not all of them *and* a wife, too." The guard chuckled. "I seen a couple of his lady friends. Real classy lookin', and I bet it takes a mountain of gold to keep them happy, too. But I'd get rid of the wife and keep any of them."

"Why doesn't he?"

"The missus is a vindictive sort, and she's got brothers. Heard-tell she don't mind her husband cattin' around as long as she's got her place in Denver society, but she'd never give him a divorce. Catholic, you know."

Slocum nodded sagely, putting together the pieces of the puzzle. Basil Aiken might have struck it rich, but his lifestyle demanded ever more money to keep his wife happy and to support a string of prostitutes. A combination like that probably included gambling and heavy drinking, though Slocum had seen no hint of that while Aiken had been in Victory. He might keep this part of his life in Denver—and the business part in other Colorado towns.

Daisy came from the back room looking stunned.

"Let's go, John." He offered her his arm as they stepped into the late afternoon sun as if leaving one world and going into another.

"So?" he asked. "Was I right?"

"There was more than ten thousand dollars in the case," she said in a hoarse whisper. "I watched Mr. Skinner count it twice. And he said it was all going into a brand-new account, one with a name on it I didn't recognize."

"To pay bills?"

Daisy held out the letter.

"I wasn't supposed to keep this, but Mr. Skinner didn't notice. What's it mean?"

Slocum glanced at it. Aiken's instructions were crystal clear—and so was his intent. He wanted an account his wife and girlfriends knew nothing about. His wife might suck him dry financially, but he was going to have a secret, untouchable account. And Daisy unknowingly had set it up for him with money taken from stock certificate sales in Victory. If Aiken's wife had her own sources of information in the bank, she would never learn of the money coming in from her husband. Slocum suspected that Aiken was paying the bank president very well for his discretion. Tellers and junior officers might tell Mrs. Aiken of surreptitious deposits, but Mr. Skinner wouldn't.

"This is the only name. It looks to be a business," Slocum said. "Consolidated Shipping."

"Perhaps Mr. Aiken is paying a freight bill," Daisy said. She sounded unsure. Everything that had come into Victory had been brought by railroad, and none of it had been ordered directly by Aiken.

"Might be Aiken's putting something aside for a rainy day," Slocum said.

Daisy didn't understand. "But it's sunny. And warm for this late in the year. Oh, well. I've done what I was sent to Denver to do. If I hurry I can catch the last train back to Victory."

Daisy looked questioningly at him, her bright blue eyes dancing with merriment.

He answered. "We can catch the last train back. I bought a round-trip ticket, too."

"You're so sweet, John, spending your own money to be my bodyguard like this. Why Mr. Aiken didn't tell me I was carrying so much money, or send Andy along to help protect it, is beyond me. But I'm glad it worked out this way."

They returned to the train station. Daisy had forgotten about the man who had tried to knife her, but Slocum hadn't. Then the whistle blasted its earsplitting shrill note, warning that the train was ready to pull out, and he put such things from his mind, too.

# 9

"What are you looking for, John?" Daisy Stevenson sat with her hands folded in her lap, looking at him out of the corner of her eye.

"Nothing," Slocum lied. He was trying to catch a glimpse of Aiken's henchman, but he had not seen the man since he'd run him off outside the Denver bank. The train already wended its way back to Victory, rattling and clanking—without the man aboard. Slocum breathed a little easier, but he had to worry about what Daisy was riding back into. If Aiken had intended her to be robbed and probably killed in Denver that meant she knew something he didn't want revealed. But the suitcase had contained a great deal of money. Why would Aiken try to have his own secret stash stolen?

Slocum was at a loss to figure what that might be since Daisy bought into the mining magnate's scheme as fully as her brother. Even now, she refused to think ill of Basil Aiken.

"Oh pish, you're worried over something. What is it, John? The money is already safely in the bank. Nobody'd want to rob me now. I hardly have two dollars left."

"What else are you doing for Aiken? What other jobs?"

Slocum was startled at the reaction. Daisy blushed and looked away, staring at the Front Range in the distance as the train worked its way southward.

"What'd he do?"

"Please, John, it might not have been like that. I might have misunderstood what he was suggesting." She smiled weakly as she turned back to him. "It's not like he's not an attractive man, but I don't think of him that way."

"He propositioned you?" Slocum did not think of Aiken as "an attractive man" and doubted Daisy would either, except for his millionaire status and the promise of making her brother rich.

"It seemed that way at first, but he convinced me I was wrong, that I misinterpreted what he said." Daisy blushed again. "It's just that my mind was elsewhere. On you."

Slocum knew she was struggling to get the subject away from Aiken and his indecent proposal to her. For this alone, Slocum would put a bullet in Aiken's heart. And Daisy saw it in his face.

"Oh, John, it's nothing. I handled it just fine. In fact, the more I think on it, the more I'm sure Mr. Aiken was right and I misinterpreted what he meant."

"How long after this happened did he decide to send you to Denver?"

"Why, I don't know. Not long. A day or two, perhaps. Then yes, he said he wanted me to bring the suitcase here. Well, Denver. You know wh-what I mean." Daisy was getting flustered again, showing how agitated she was over Aiken. She reached out and put her hand on Slocum's. He started to pull back, then stopped. She needed his support because she was out of her depth dealing with a slick operator like Basil Aiken. The best Slocum could guess, when Daisy had turned Aiken down, he had concocted a scheme to get rid of her and make it appear that it was nothing but a robbery turned violent.

Slocum wondered what else Aiken might have gotten

from Daisy's death and the loss of the money. Payment to his wife would have been lost, but there'd be an explanation for it. And his mistresses might also be content with the explanation of thievery in their hometown. The icing on the cake would be Aiken putting the supposedly stolen money into his pocket.

As it was, the botched robbery-and-murder attempt didn't affect anything. Had Aiken taken the possibility of his henchman's failure into account? Slocum thought it was possible. Aiken was a crafty character and left nothing to chance. Daisy wasn't hard to read; Aiken might know she wouldn't pursue the matter of his amorous advances. And Aiken's wife and mistresses got their money. He wasn't out that much, unless Daisy rocked the boat.

But why had he sent the letter creating a sham account with Daisy?

"He's a skunk," Slocum said. "He's running a swindle on you, on Andy, on everyone in Victory."

"Why don't you like him, John? Mr. Aiken's not a bad sort. He might be a bit ruthless, but he's quite successful. Successful men are like that." Daisy spoke with determination, as if this was the only way a rich man could be. Slocum didn't know. She might be right. That still didn't excuse Aiken's behavior—or the possibility he had tried to kill the woman.

"Sell some of the stock certificates and get even," Slocum urged. "That's not so much to ask. If the value of what you have left goes way up, you'll still be rich."

"Mr. Aiken explained it to Andy. Every single share of stock matters. We're piling it up and will be rich, John. Are you against that? We're not hurting anyone. In fact, if we get rich, so does everyone else in Victory. Everyone who has bought shares in the Mother Lode Mine and gone out and worked hard and actually dug up gold on their own, too."

Slocum gave up. He could never convince Daisy how

Aiken and his men were swindling the entire town. Even if she found out on her own how Aiken had bought into most of the stores to suck up the profits made selling equipment to the rush of miners come to get rich, she'd only chalk it up to clever business sense.

"I'll be moving on when we get back to Victory," he said. "There's not much more I can do there."

Slocum saw the blonde's face seem to melt and tears well in the corners of her eyes.

"No, you can't. Stay, please stay. I-I'll miss y-you." The stutter returned, showing her agitation.

Slocum was adamant. He couldn't protect her if she insisted nothing was wrong and that she was prospering. It would be a hard lesson for her to learn eventually, and Slocum wasn't sure he wanted to be around when she and her brother did learn not to trust men with stories that were too good to be true. If he wanted to be a nursemaid, he'd find himself a sick calf and nurse it back to health. At least there'd be some good beef in the offing.

"Go on, you ride off. If you do, I'll come after you!"

This startled Slocum.

"I'll have enough money to follow you to the ends of the earth. And I'll show you how wrong you are!"

He saw fire and determination and all the other traits that had drawn him to Daisy Stevenson in the first place.

"You do that," he said. "Something tells me I won't be able to ride far enough, fast enough to avoid you—even if I did want to get away."

He saw resolve come to her eyes, resolve and not a bit of mischievousness. She squeezed harder on his hand and tugged a little, indicating he should stand up.

"I've got a sleeping berth. It's getting mighty dark out."

"Not that dark," he said, teasing her now.

"Plenty dark enough for me to get sleepy enough to go to bed."

"It's dark in those berths?" asked Slocum. "It might be scary, if it's too dark."

"I'd certainly need someone to hold, to keep close—real close." Her tongue slipped out between her lips, just enough so the tip made a slow, wet circuit over her ruby lips. Between this overt gesture and the way her hand had moved to his crotch and squeezed down gently, there was no mistaking her intent.

She stood and brushed past him, leaning forward just enough so her breasts, hidden under her crisply starched white blouse, danced tantalizingly in front of Slocum's face. He looked up and saw that Daisy was flushed again, but this time it was not from embarrassment.

He let her past. When she got into the aisle, she bent down and whispered, "I've left my purse." With that she straightened and walked steadily toward the rear so she could pass into the sleeping berths in the last passenger car.

Slocum waited a few minutes, anticipating what was to come. He found his mind racing ahead faster than the train itself as he ran his fingers over the beadwork on her purse. She had left it as an excuse for him to follow, as if he needed one—or anyone else on the train cared what they did. Most slept on the hard seats, hats pulled low over their faces. The two other women sat side by side, whispering about who knew what. Slocum stood and made a show of the purse falling to the floor. He said nothing but picked it up and looked around, as if only then realizing its owner had left.

Without hurrying he made his way to the rear. The train hit a patch of rough track, forcing him to brace himself repeatedly to keep from getting tossed around. They were hurtling past Colorado City on their way south along the Front Range. A lovely sight, but Slocum knew an even lovelier one awaited him in the next car.

He stopped at the door leading to the rear car and

looked at the passengers. No one took notice of him—or Daisy. Slocum quickly opened the door, swung onto the small platform between cars, then entered the sleeping car and stopped dead in his tracks. He had thought Daisy had a small cabin with a bunk in it. The bunks lined the corridor, separated only by dangling blankets to afford some privacy. Anyone in another bunk or coming along the aisle could hear them.

More than this, Slocum didn't know which berth Daisy was in. He might wander along, peeking into each but that might get a six-shooter shoved into his face. It would definitely create a commotion he didn't want.

He considered the problem for a moment, then studied the train floor. Dust and soot had poured in from the doors at either end of the car every time they opened. The only fresh tracks were small, showing a quick step, as if the person was eager to get to her destination. Slocum smiled. He was eager, too.

The tracks ended halfway down the aisle and turned right. That eliminated all but two bunks. Up or down? That proved easier than Slocum had thought. Daisy had gone up on her toes which meant she had pulled herself into the top bunk. Slocum went to the berth and pulled back the curtain.

"Why, sir, you expose me!" Daisy sat in the bunk, naked as far as Slocum could see. She made no move to pull up the sheet to cover her firm, proud breasts.

"Then I'd better do something about covering you, ma'am," Slocum said. He hopped up into the berth and sat for a moment with his legs dangling. "This is going to be a tight fit."

"I certainly hope so," Daisy said. All trace of her hesitation and insecurity had vanished.

Slocum laughed and hiked his feet up into the berth. As he turned, Daisy's hands snaked around him and began pulling off his shirt. He kicked free of his boots while she worked on his gun belt—and more. Her nimble fingers stroked down over his crotch where the bulge was growing larger by the second. The nearness of the woman, the smell of her soft blond hair, the satiny feel of her breasts rubbing against his back, the tight, taut nipples poking into his flesh, all excited Slocum more and more.

By the time Daisy got the buttons on his fly open he was about ready to scream. It came as a rush of relief when his manhood popped free of the cloth prison and into the warm circle of the woman's fingers. She began stroking up and down, cooing like a dove.

"Soooo nice," she whispered hotly in his ear, then lightly nipped at it. "And so hard."

"All for you," Slocum said.

"I don't think so," Daisy said. "I think a lot of this is for you. And that's the way I want it!" She tightened her grip and began moving her hand up and down faster. Slocum sucked in his breath and let the sensations wash through him. The woman's hot breath in his ear was quickly followed by her darting pink tongue. The feel of her chest pressing into his back thrilled him, but it was the way her hand moved that kept him occupied the most.

He leaned back, forcing Daisy to lie down. Her hand never left his throbbing length. Slocum twisted about, and Daisy reluctantly let him go free. For a moment. The instant he was lying atop her, the woman's hand slipped between their bodies and found her fleshy grip again.

"That's not a pump handle, ma'am," he said. "You don't have to pump it up and down so hard."

"No, it's already nice and hard, but who knows what might come spewing out if I keep pumping?"

"You know what'd come out," he said, kissing her to cut off such silly talk. Their lips met and melted together. This sent both of their passions soaring. Daisy released her grip and brought her hands around so she could run them over

Slocum's broad, muscular back. For his part, he loved the feel of her hard nubs poking into his chest. He loved it so much he had to have more.

Slocum wiggled about a little and caught one cherry-bright nip in his lips. He sucked hard. This brought a gasp of delight to Daisy's lips. The blonde struggled beneath him, but he held her in place with only his lips. Then he added his tongue and lightly nipped with his teeth. Daisy's legs spread wide and she locked her ankles behind his back, but he wasn't in position.

He was enjoying his oral exploration too much at the moment to think of other pursuits.

He pulled back a little and toyed with her blood-engorged nipple using his tongue, flicking it about like a rattler sampling the air. When he felt the throb of the woman's heart through the teat, he moved to the other crest where he found an equally rigid cap atop the mound of quivering flesh. He buried his face between the twin mountains and kissed, licked and moved lower, intending to kiss between her legs.

The confines of the sleeping berth prevented it.

"John, no, come back. It's not possible."

Slocum usually rose to a challenge, but he saw she was right. He was bumping against the ceiling of the bunk and there wasn't room enough to move any lower, even with her knees drawn up so she exposed herself fully to him. Slocum snaked his way back up, touching here and there, kissing and licking and finally reaching her luscious lips once more.

Only in this position could he move himself into place. He felt the tip of his manhood knocking on Daisy's carnal doors, but the rolling of the train kept him from entering until she reached between them and guided him forward.

The train hit a rough patch of track and Slocum slammed forward, sinking full-length into the woman. The sudden intrusion might have hurt. But the woman was already more than prepared for him. He slid slickly and crushed down on her, entirely hidden within her female sheath.

"Oh, oh," was all the blonde could gasp out.

Slocum felt the same. Words jumbled in his throat. Emotion tore at all logic, all sense disappeared and left him an animal in rut. He looked down into the woman's face. Her blue eyes were closed and her face was a mask of equally animal desire. She wanted all-out lovemaking and nothing less would do.

Slocum did not move. He remained buried within the warm, moist tunnel.

"More, more," Daisy grated out. "Move!"

Slocum did not move. He twitched his hips and worked to control his own instincts to do as the woman urged. The tightness surrounding him aroused him and sent lightning bolts of desire throughout his loins. But he didn't move. Even when Daisy lifted her legs and again locked her heels behind his back, he did not move. He let the rolling motion of the train furnish what small motion he conveyed to the moaning blonde beneath him.

"More, more," she begged, then let the begging trail off as she began to appreciate what Slocum was doing. The train furnished vibration as well as rocking movement. She gripped harder and her legs tensed around him, drawing him down even more firmly.

But as exotic and exciting as this was, nature overrode Slocum's control and forced him to twitch. Just a little. Then he could no longer restrain his impulses. He forced his hips back against the powerful legs holding him in place, then levered forward. An inch. Two. Back. The next time he stroked more deeply and withdrew more. She took him entirely into her molten core where he rested for only a moment before withdrawing slowly, teasingly, intoxicatingly.

Soon, with the rolling motion of the train adding to his impetus, he drove hard and deep giving them both the stimulation that had been lacking. Friction mounted and the noise of steel wheels against railroad tracks mingled with the sight of the woman and the smell of their arousal and the heat of the moment.

Slocum grunted as he felt the surge along his rigid length. Daisy rolled up into an even tighter ball and squeezed down powerfully on him, milking him as her own ecstasy whirled through her like a prairie tornado. Locked together, struggling, moving, grating and gliding, they finally exhausted their passions and lay limp as dishrags, arms wrapped around one another.

"That was so . . ."

"Good?" Slocum suggested.

"Great!"

Slocum and Daisy lay alongside one another, the berth weighed down dangerously. Slocum wondered if anyone lay in the bunk beneath. If so, they might find themselves all together soon. But he didn't worry about that. The feel of the woman's naked, sweaty flesh against his as the train raced southward, back to Victory, was good enough.

For the moment. Slocum knew he had a big decision to make when they got to town. Did he ride on? Or did he do something about Basil Aiken and his swindling ways?

# 10

The train pulled into Victory a little after dawn. Slocum let Daisy Stevenson leave first. He followed so he could see Basil Aiken's surprise if the mining magnate happened to be on the depot platform waiting. It was too early in the morning for such a rich and powerful man to be out and about, Slocum decided, but not for his minions. Andy Stevenson greeted his sister warmly, then abruptly turned from her to try to sell other disembarking passengers stock certificates in the Mother Lode Mine.

Slocum shook his head. The man was untiring, unceasing, an elemental force of nature when it came to peddling the worthless pieces of paper. If he only applied himself in some gainful fashion, he could be rich.

Hanging back a bit farther as Daisy made her way down the boardwalk heading for her cabin, Slocum kept an eye peeled for any of Aiken's other henchmen. He wanted to see their reaction to Daisy's safe and sound return. He was disappointed when he didn't spot any of them.

"Hey, Slocum, you gonna pay for another week in the livery?" called Smitty, the stable owner. Smitty hoisted a whiskey bottle and drained the last of it. "I got me a long list of folks wantin' me to put up their horses. The whole danged town is bustin' at the seams with newcomers. And that no-good hired hand of mine upped and went out lookin' fer gold, after all I tole him about how dumb it was."

Slocum sauntered over to where the livery owner sat in front of the Sweetwater Saloon and dropped into the empty chair beside him.

"Business must be good, if you can take the time to sit and yell at people in the street," Slocum said.

The man grinned crookedly and nodded. "You don't know the half of it, Slocum. There's a couple dozen new faces a day showin' up in town. Marshal Borrega's goin' crazy tryin' to keep track of them all. He's absolutely sure some must be outlaws on the run, tryin' to hide in the crowd."

"Might be right," Slocum allowed. He wondered if there might not be a wanted poster with his own likeness on it under the stack of papers on the marshal's desk. He hadn't led the purest of lives since coming West after shooting a carpetbagger judge who had taken a fancy to the family farm back in Calhoun, Georgia. The lying Yankee judge had said no taxes had been paid on Slocum's Stand and that he was seizing it for nonpayment. He'd gotten more real estate than he'd bargained for—about six-by-two-by-six worth. Him and his hired gun should never have crossed John Slocum. But killing a federal judge, even one who deserved it, was against the law and Slocum had dodged that particular warrant for a considerable time.

But that was hardly his only transgression of the law. It was just the one he had the hardest time shaking loose from.

"You makin' money off them?" asked the stable owner. He gestured vaguely down Victory's main street.

"Can't say that I am. I'm thinking of moving on."

The livery owner turned and stared at him as if he had grown three heads.

"You're joshin' me, aren't you? You ain't gonna leave a purty filly like Miss Stevenson. Never seen a decent woman who was better lookin', and from what I kin tell she takes a fancy to you, too."

Slocum wasn't about to discuss his personal affairs with the owner of a livery stable who whiled away his spare time sitting in front of a saloon, waiting for it to open. But this was the kind of man who missed nothing in town, in spite of his drunkenness. From what Slocum could tell, Smitty's demeanor depended a great deal on how much— or how little—booze he had imbibed.

"What's Aiken been up to since I was out of town?" asked Slocum.

The livery owner picked at his teeth with a splinter of wood from the saloon wall, then spat.

"Tried to buy into my business, he did. Wouldn't hear of it. He got downright nasty. Seems he's part owner of danged near every business in this place."

"Reckon the gold mining will pay off?"

"Never does," the man opined. "I seen what happened back in Denver in '59. Lots of excitement, lots of people, never enough gold to go around. Oh, some struck it rich."

"Aiken did," Slocum said.

"Couple times over, but men like that, well, they never get enough."

"How many men're working for him? Other than Stevenson?"

"Stevenson and his sister, you mean?" The livery owner laughed. "Best I kin tell, from what animals they put up at my stables, Touhy and a pair of others. That's all. Don't like that Clyde Touhy. Nasty son of a gun."

"Who're the others?"

"Randall or Ransom or something like that's the mean-est one." He pondered the matter for a minute, then de-clared, "Name's Randall. Fer gosh certain, that's it. Got that glint in his eye what makes you leery of ever turnin' yer back on him. The other's 'fraid of his own shadow. His name's Zach. Never heard more 'n that."

"Seen Randall the past couple days?"

"Now that you mention it, nope, ain't seen hide nor hair of him. And his horse's in the stall next to yours, so he ain't been ridin' around. Might be he's hunkered down up at the Mother Lode Mine, guardin' it. Heard-tell of some claim-jumpers wanting to elbow their way in. Touhy took care of 'em, he did. He's got a mean streak, too, but not like Randall's."

Slocum nodded. Any man who could try to knife a woman on a Denver street was more than mean. He was a rabid killer who had to be put out of his misery.

"Might be able to use a spare hand at the stables, Slocum," the liveryman said, looking at him with bloodshot eyes. "Don't know if you're lookin' for work, but I need help with all the eager prospectors comin' to town. Some don't pay their bill, so I take their animal and need somebody knowledgeable to get a good price. You've worked cattle, I suspect, maybe been around ranches running horses, too."

"I have," Slocum admitted. He had wondered why Smitty was cozying up to him the way he was. Now it was obvious. The stable owner wanted Slocum's help after losing his stable hand to the gold fields.

"You can keep half of ever'thing you make sellin' the horses and mules. Might not be much at first, but with the flood of men into Victory, it's got to increase."

Slocum considered his options. He still had a bankroll in his pocket but with boomtown prices he was less likely by the day to afford to live here. The thought came to him that he had considered drifting on and now he was thinking about how to live in a town where food prices would soar. Slocum laughed ruefully. He had come to a decision what to do about Daisy—about Daisy and her brother and the others in Victory—and hadn't known it until this instant.

"That's a mighty generous offer," Slocum said. "I'd take you up on it, except for one thing."

"What's that?" the livery owner said suspiciously. "I can't offer you a salary. You got to earn what you make from me."

"I don't know if I'd make enough on any given day to put up my own horse. I'd hate to be in the position of having to sell my own horse."

The stable owner laughed and shoved out his calloused hand.

"You kin board that roan of yers fer free, you bandit!"

"Glad to be working with you, Smitty," Slocum said, shaking his hand.

"The way things're goin' right about now, you come on back at sundown and I'll have two swayback mules and a decent riding horse fer you to peddle."

"Sounds good since I have business to attend to."

"Betcha I know what her name is, too." Smitty gave a broad wink. Then he shot to his feet. The doors to the Sweetwater Saloon were swung wide open and he hurried inside. He called back to Slocum, "See you at sunset. Don't you go gettin' into too much trouble 'cuz I ain't gonna bail you out of Marshal Borrega's jail."

"I won't get into that kind of trouble." Slocum listened to Smitty's appreciative laugh and then heaved himself to his feet and headed down the street toward the storefront where Basil Aiken had set up the Mother Lode Mine office. Aiken had done well with the once-abandoned building. The plateglass window sported gilt lettering telling the world whose office this was. Aiken's desk stood in the center of the window so the man could look out into the street and anyone passing by could see him. The interior was simply decorated but done with expensive furniture, giving everyone a hint of how they could live when they struck it rich, too.

With stock in the Mother Lode Mine.

Slocum started to walk past but slowed and then found himself a spot across the street where he could watch Aiken inside. The man read and reread a telegram, then crumpled it and tossed it onto his desk where it stood out like a yellow wart. Aiken's expression was one of fury, but he quickly covered it when Daisy Stevenson opened the door and went in. Watching closely, Slocum saw how hard Aiken worked to keep from showing his previous anger. He smiled insincerely and spoke in what looked to be short, precise sentences while Daisy spoke at length.

Aiken finally rose, shook her hand from across the desk and dropped her hand as if it were fiery hot. He then gave her a book like the one her brother used to dispense receipts and write stock certificates for buyers in the Mother Lode Mine. Daisy did a little curtsey and left, clutching the book. Her expression as she came out was one of excitement.

Aiken's had returned to fury. He slammed a meaty hand onto the desk, causing everything on it to bounce. Then he took out a lucifer, struck it on the edge of his desk and put the flame to the telegram. Slocum watched as the flimsy yellow paper turned to ash instantly. With a dismissive sweep of his arm, Basil Aiken cleaned off the desk and sent the debris floating throughout the office.

Slocum waited a few more minutes but when Aiken calmed and turned his attention to working in ledger books, he knew he would see nothing more of interest. Slocum had been heading toward Daisy's cabin but now he chose a different destination. He cut over a street and down a block to the telegraph office, near the railroad depot.

"Good day, sir," the telegrapher said, looking up from his contraption. Huge vats of acid with lead plates shoved into them had been wired together and connected to the key at one time, but now the telegrapher had it all taken apart.

"I'd wanted to send a telegram, but it doesn't look as if anything's coming in or going out," said Slocum.

"I can take the message and get it out in an hour or two."

"Doesn't look as if anything's come in for hours," Slocum said.

"Nope, sure hasn't. Late yesterday afternoon was the last 'gram I got 'fore things got busted. Damn batteries." The telegrapher thumped one of the glass containers with his thumbnail.

"That'd have been the telegram for Mr. Aiken, wouldn't it?"

"Was," the telegrapher said, then looked up suspiciously. "How'd you know?"

"Came in from Denver." This was a guess on Slocum's part but not too farfetched a one. The man Smitty had identified as Aiken's henchman, Randall, was most likely the one who had sent it. Slocum was sorry he hadn't killed the man when he had the chance.

"How can I help you, mister?" The telegrapher stripped off his rubber apron and came over to the counter. His hands were acid-burned and his eyes were tiny dark dots fixed on Slocum now, as if Slocum would cause trouble of some unknown kind.

"I'll need a telegram blank," Slocum said.

"Here it is," the man said, reaching under the counter. "I'll fill it out for you. Just dictate what you want to send, who's to receive it and the destination."

"I can write it out," Slocum said.

The telegrapher looked at him with disdain.

"I'm gonna see it when I send it. I got to read it, you know, so there's no secrets."

"Right," Slocum said. "I want—damn, it's spilling all over the floor!" he pointed to the table where the telegrapher had been working on the acid batteries. Pointing was all it took to get the man to whirl around.

"What? What're you talking about?"

"Leaking. All over the floor. In back. Can't you smell it?" Slocum knew the man's sense of smell would have been dimmed by his proximity to the acid.

"I don't—" The telegrapher left the counter to get a better look where Slocum pointed. As he went, Slocum reached down and flipped back a page in the book. He caught a glimpse of the telegram Aiken had received and it had been sent by Randall. While he failed to fully decipher the telegrapher's crabbed writing, he got a sense of what Randall had sent from Denver.

Slocum understood why Aiken had been so mad when he read the telegram. Randall had reported his failure to kill Daisy.

"You got rocks in your head. There's nothing wrong." The telegrapher turned back, suspicious. But Slocum had turned the telegram copy book back and looked as innocent as he could. "You want to give me the 'gram now?"

"I'll be back when you get that rig fixed," Slocum said. He stepped out into the street, worrying about Daisy's safety. Randall was still back in Denver but Touhy was still here and had a mean streak Aiken could use to good advantage. And the other one, Randall's partner when he had salted the Mother Lode Mine. Slocum struggled to remember what Smitty had called him.

"Zach," he said. "That's all the name he knew." Slocum began walking along the street, thinking hard. Either Zach or Touhy could easily stab Daisy and make it look like robbery if she was selling stock certificates for the mine. The only benefit was that Daisy might stay in public and be relatively safe, but eventually she had to leave the crowds and head back to her lonely cabin.

"Andy!" Slocum shouted to the young man who stood on a street corner hawking the stock certificates. Slocum waved and got the man's attention.

"Mr. Slocum, haven't seen you around for a while."

Slocum wasn't sure if Stevenson had noticed his sister had been gone the same length of time or if he was only making conversation. Andy Stevenson was too focused on selling bogus stock for Aiken to be aware of much happening around him.

That would have to change. Fast.

"Just heard something mighty disturbing," Slocum said. "Your sister's working for Aiken now, selling stock, just like you."

"I'm mighty proud of her," Stevenson said.

"Rumor around town is that a couple hard cases intend to rob her, maybe hurt her bad."

"Who?"

"You know how it is with rumors in a saloon," Slocum said, doubting Andy did. "No names, but where there's smoke, there's fire. I'd take it real serious, if I were you."

"But she can't stop selling the stock certificates. That's how we're going to get rich."

"Work with her, don't let her out of your sight. And be ready for a couple owlhoots trying to rob her. Since you're both doing the same thing now, it shouldn't be hard to throw in together."

"But we can cover more of the town by splitting up," Stevenson said. Then it finally penetrated what Slocum was saying. "I'm not going to let her endanger herself, not for our future. I can sell plenty by myself."

"Good man," Slocum said, slapping Stevenson on the shoulder. He wondered if the young man was a little dim. Even if he was, he understood the peril his sister faced.

"Where are you going? You can help watch after her."

"I'd like to," said Slocum, "but I've got to leave town for a day or two. Maybe longer, but I doubt it."

"Where are you going?"

"To see some men about a mine," Slocum said. He had to stay around Victory until he saw how many horses and mules Smitty had to sell, but he could be on the trail soon afterward. It might not be too bad an idea to take a couple spare horses with him, where he was going.

# 11

Slocum rode into the Ute camp with three horses Smitty
had confiscated for nonpayment of stabling fees. With
some clever trading and not a little bit of desperation on
the part of a half-dozen prospectors, Slocum had sold the
mules he had for enough to cover the price of the horses.
Slocum had then ridden into the Ute camp with three
horses and rode out with only his roan and a big smile on
his face.

The Ute hunting chief, Bear Tail, still used the knife
Slocum had given him when they had met before. And now
Slocum had a better idea where to wander through the hills
west of Victory and what to look for.

He rode to the top of a ridge and looked down over a
quiet valley. It'd make good grazing range, but the Utes
had hunted here for generations and wouldn't take kindly
to intrusion. They wouldn't have much choice, Slocum
knew. The onslaught of white men hunting for gold would
be too powerful a wave to hold back. The Indians might as
well try to grab air in their hands and carry it away.

Slocum consulted a compass he had brought from town,
squinted to get the angle of the sun and then consulted a
crude map the land office had provided him. While better

than nothing, it was vague. This would only cause big trouble in the near future when one claim intruded on another as the prospectors became more frantic to find what Slocum doubted was even here.

He adjusted the map, got his bearings and rode down the gentle slope into the valley where a stream ran from higher in the mountains. He jumped to the ground and poked around a bit, then set about putting up stone cairns and put his claim to the land in a baking powder can. Taking one last ride around his newly staked claim, Slocum studied the area nearby and nodded slowly as things came together.

It took the better part of the day to ride back to Victory, but he spent the time thinking and plotting and planning. His confidence was high when he dismounted in front of the land office and got in a line that stretched from the front door, past the Sweetwater Saloon and a goodly ten yards beyond down the street.

"Looks like they're doing a brisk business," Slocum said to the dandy in front of him. The man was dressed more for a game of faro in a gambling salon than for grubbing in the hard rock of a mountainside.

"Yes, sir, they are. And I intend to stake out my claim and make a fortune."

"How're you going to do that?" asked Slocum. The question caused the well-groomed man's eyebrows to rise. Then he laughed.

"You are a man of great discernment, I see. I am filing land deeds with the intention of selling them to newcomers."

"Didn't think you'd cotton much to swinging a pick."

"Good Lord, no! The real money is always to be had selling to the prospectors, not clawing the metal from the ground. If there is any gold to be had."

"You think Basil Aiken's wrong this time? You know the man? His reputation?"

"Of course I know Basil," the man said, smoothing

wrinkles from his jacket. "He has had great success in the past. Perhaps he will here, also. Would you like to purchase some land from me? Land he has spoken of as holding vast veins of golden ore?"

"I'll pass," Slocum said. He recognized this man as a vulture swooping in to pick up the crumbs left by Aiken. The difference between Victory and most boomtowns was that Slocum doubted Aiken would leave few crumbs for anyone else to peck at.

They moved slowly until Slocum got to the county clerk. The man had bloodshot eyes and looked as if he were ready to fly off the handle. His hand shook as he dipped the pen into the inkwell and poised it above the page, ready to record what Slocum told him.

"You ain't tryin' to do like that feller in front of you and register every last inch of land in the whole danged county, are you?"

"Here," Slocum said, passing over a slip of paper with the information the clerk needed. The man looked skeptical, took the paper and peered shortsightedly at it.

"Oh, you're the one what scouted for Andy Stevenson when he staked out the Mother Lode Mine. So you know these things. Good. Glad to see someone with all their ducks in a row." The man scribbled furiously, blotted and then announced, "That's two dollars. And here's your deed."

Slocum paid, checked the deed to be sure the clerk had recorded the proper plot of land and then asked, "You have a map showing what all's been claimed?"

"I do, but it's not up-to-date. This mornin' alone I filed more 'n fifty claims. I'll be up till midnight getting everything transferred onto the map."

"I'm only interested in the Mother Lode Mine claim."

"Heck, we got extra copies of that. Compliments of Mr. Aiken."

"Why didn't I think of that?" Slocum said. His sarcasm was lost on the clerk, who fumbled under the counter and brought out a ream of paper. He used a penknife to cut the twine and handed a sheet to Slocum.

"This is what I want. It gives the precise locations of the boundary lines."

"Good hunting. Hope you strike it as rich as the rest of us."

"You have to be making a young fortune recording all this," Slocum said as he started to leave. He heart turned to ice when he heard the clerk's answer.

"This is only a temporary job. I'm pourin' every penny of my salary and savings into stock certificates in the Mother Lode Mine. I'm gettin' rich, just like the rest of this here town, and Aiken's the one who'll do it for me."

Slocum stepped into the cool autumn afternoon and took a deep breath. There might be a hint of storm coming in, but the sky was clear and there was hardly a zephyr stirring. He walked to the general store and stopped outside when he saw a dozen men struggling to pile up sheets of canvas.

"What're those for?" he called.

One of the workers looked up as he wiped sweat from his face. He obviously sought any excuse to take a break and came over.

"Got a trainload of canvas in this afternoon. Freight train, it was. Don't see many of them in Victory, not usually. Mr. Aiken, he figgered housing would be in short supply so we got this tent-makin' material. Sellin' it like there's no tomorrow. Already got four new saloons usin' the canvas, not to mention a small town of prospectors on the far side. Goin' to be a big town 'fore we know it."

"Tent city," Slocum mused. He had to hand it to Aiken. The man cut this pie every way to Sunday. He had bought into most stores and now was dictating what supplies to carry. Because he had done this before, the items delivering the most return for the least dollar were all that would come in on the trains under his aegis.

"Beats where I'm livin' and I been here six months," the

man said. "Kin I help you with something? I recognize you as the man what helped Andy Stevenson prove the Mother Lode Mine."

"Prove it?"

"You and him staked it out and then got back with all that gold. 'Course, that Clyde Touhy helped. That's why he was up there on the stage, but I heard the truth. You and Stevenson found lumps of gold bigger 'n my fist. That's what got Mr. Aiken so excited about the Mother Lode."

"Bigger than a fist," Slocum mused.

"I *knew* it! It wasn't just a rumor. Well, sir, what can I get for you? You have a hot new property in your sights?"

"Even better than the Mother Lode Mine," Slocum solemnly assured the man. He gave an abbreviated list of what he'd need and was surprisingly given credit at the store.

"You keep me in mind now, when you strike it rich," the man said. "My father-in-law's the one what owns the store, and I don't intend workin' my ass off for him the rest of my born days."

"Gold," Slocum said vaguely.

"That's what it takes. Gold!"

Content, the man went back to stacking the mountains of canvas as Slocum wrestled with his purchases, loaded them on his horse and rode out of town. He rode smack down the middle of the main street, loudly greeting people as he left. The pick and pan bounced prominently against his saddlebags and he made no secret that he had registered a claim at the land office. Before Victory lay at his back, Slocum had informed almost everyone in town of his good fortune.

Somewhere prior to midnight he reached his now-registered claim. He dropped the supplies under a pine tree and tended his horse before stretching out his blanket and collapsing. It had been a long, hard day, but he was happy with all he had done. With the stream gurgling peacefully a dozen yards away, Slocum drifted off to sleep, only to come awake an hour before sunrise, his Colt Navy clutched in his hand.

He had reacted before consciously identifying the reason for his sudden awakening. Straining, he listened hard. Nothing. Then he caught the faint odor of tobacco. Somewhere upwind a man smoked a cigarette. Slocum turned slowly and homed in on the source of the tobacco smoke and caught sight of a glowing red coal in the darkness.

After strapping on his gun belt and shoving his six-shooter into it, he reached for his Winchester. Rolling onto his belly, he carefully sighted in on where the man so carelessly smoking would be standing. Slocum's finger came back slowly on the rifle trigger, then he paused. Whoever was out there would have attacked straightaway unless he was waiting for something. Or someone.

Slocum twisted around and tried to locate another ambusher in the trees and undergrowth around him. If one was out there, he was more expert at hiding himself than his partner. His rifle came back and centered on the spot where the smoker's face would be.

"Come on out," Slocum called. At the same instant he pulled the trigger. The Winchester kicked him in the shoulder, and he was rewarded with the sight of the cigarette coal flying in an arc through the night. But the shot felt wrong. He wasn't sure he hit anyone.

The silence was relieved only by the softly murmuring stream. All night animals had fallen silent at the gunshot. Even the wind was gone, leaving behind a blanket of chilly mountain air that refused to stir. Slocum knew better than to rush out to see if a body lay at the base of the tree where the man had stood. He levered another round into the rifle chamber and waited. And waited.

He had learned great patience during the war when he had served as a sniper for the CSA. Some days he had spent fifteen hours in the crook of a tree, as unmoving as the limb where he rested, hoping to catch the momentary flash of sunlight on a Yankee officer's braid. More than once his single shot had robbed the enemy of its leader at a crucial moment. But now patience served no purpose.

Exposed as he was, it might give his attackers time to get him in a cross fire. Wiggling forward like a snake, Slocum headed for the stream. The instant he did so, he heard movement behind him, men rushing into camp. From the intensity of the footfalls, he guessed he faced at least three men. He rolled onto his back and swung his rifle around, firing when he saw a dark silhouette against the night sky.

The instant he fired a foot-long tongue of orange licked his way. The lead dug up a small hole beside his hip. His round was better aimed. The owlhoot trying to kill him threw up his hands. For a brief second a new flame blasted skyward and then the outlaw collapsed to the ground. The slug he had fired into the air in his death throes whined off, never to be heard again.

Slocum rolled and rolled again, this time splashing into the stream. From here he was more exposed but he also had a better look at the ground in the direction of his campsite where the other outlaws gathered to kill him. The noise he made entering the water betrayed his exact location. Bullets danced all around, forcing him to run for it. Half slipping, half running, he charged upstream.

A sudden pain in his wrist caused him to drop his rifle. A bullet had grazed him. He flopped down onto his belly again, fished the rifle from the stream, then cast it aside. He couldn't fire it without risking the barrel blowing up. The muzzle had dug down into silt and sand at the bottom of the stream. The rifle wasn't safe for use until after a thorough cleaning.

Slocum hoped he was still around to perform such a chore.

He wondered at the men after him. By now most outlaws would be whooping and hollering, shouting curses and accusations at one another because they hadn't managed to gun him down in his sleep. There was nothing to betray the remaining gunmen. He didn't even have a clear notion if he faced two men or more. The one he had plugged was out of the fight—permanently. But the thunder of feet running into his camp had been loud enough that there might have been four bushwhackers. He just didn't know.

Slocum veered away from the stream and immediately regretted it. His boots made sucking sounds as he moved, and the *drip-drip-drip* of water from his clothing was loud enough to wake the dead. Whether he moved or stood stock-still, he made noise. Crouching, Slocum drew his six-shooter and waited. He knew the ambushers would come to him. And they did.

More rounds whined through the night, but they weren't close to him. Slocum suspected the men—two from the muzzle flashes—were trying to flush him like a quail. They moved their field of fire closer to him. One hunk of lead passed within inches of his ear, leaving him slightly deaf. But Slocum remained as immobile as any granite statue.

Only when he had a decent shot did he fire. His .36 caliber round sounded feeble compared to the outlaws' larger caliber weapons. The result was just as deadly. The dark blob he had shot into sagged and dropped. Slocum imagined seeing the outlaw go to his knees, clutching his side. A second round about where the man's head ought to be finished him.

Two down, but how many to go? Slocum knew of at least one more but there could be others. And who had sent them? Aiken?

A flurry of bullets preceded a mad frontal assault by the third outlaw. Slocum fired repeatedly but came up empty before landing a single round. Instinctively he reached for the knife in his boot top, only to find emptiness. He had given the knife to Bear Tail. Then all such self-recrimination vanished as he was bowled over by a smelly, powerful body that carried him backward and flat on the ground.

Kicking upward with his feet, Slocum maintained enough momentum to throw his attacker to one side. They grappled, rolling over and over, each trying to gain the upper hand. A bit of luck decided the matter. Slocum winced as a sharp rock poked into his back, but he jerked hard, twisted and brought the outlaw's forehead smack down on that same rock. A sick crunch echoed through the still night. Then there was only the soft gurgling of the stream.

Slocum lay panting harshly until he got his breath back. He grabbed the man's shirt and rolled him over. From the crazy way the man's head lolled, his neck had been broken when Slocum slammed his face into the rock. It had been a fluke, but that hardly mattered. The man was dead.

Dragging him a few feet, Slocum knelt and waited. If there was a fourth man out there, he would betray himself. After a few minutes of normal sounds returning to the countryside, Slocum figured he was again alone. He finished pulling the man into camp, then got the other two and laid them side by side.

Not once during the fight had any of them called to their partners for help. Slocum fanned a twig into a small torch and studied their faces. He had never seen them before in his life. A quick search of their pockets turned up less than seven dollars in silver coins and nothing to identify them. Only then did he go find where they had tethered their horses. Three. He had finished off three claim-jumpers. If that's what they were. Conjuring up a scene with Basil Aiken pounding on his fancy desk and ordering Slocum killed did nothing to prove these men worked for the mining magnate.

Although bone-tired, Slocum stripped the bodies of anything valuable and tossed it all into a burlap bag which he slung over the hindquarters of one horse. Then he got his shovel and began digging three graves. It was an hour after sunrise when he finished burying them and could head back to Victory.

•

# 12

Marshal Borrega jumped a foot when Slocum dumped the heavily laden burlap bag onto his desk.

"What's all this?" the lawman asked suspiciously, reaching up and nervously fingering his badge. "We ain't got no lost and found."

"The gents who wore the guns were trying to kill me in my sleep."

"Why'd they want to do that?" Marshal Borrega's eyes went wide as he finally studied Slocum more closely and saw the set to his jaw, the steely glint in the cold emerald eyes, and the worn handle of the Colt in what was a gunfighter's holster. "You have a feud goin' with them?"

"Don't know who they were—other than claim-jumpers. I staked out a claim and the next thing I know, they're trying to fill me full of lead."

"In your sleep?"

Slocum said nothing.

"You kilt all three of them while you was sleepin'?"

"They got careless. That happens to claim-jumpers when they think they're up against a greenhorn."

Borrega opened the bag and rummaged about inside. His eyes grew even wider when he saw the six-shooters and the few belongings, including the silver coins Slocum had found.

"You brung it all in?"

"All but their bodies. Those are buried under a tree on my claim. No markers, but if you want to dig them up and check to see if my story rings true, do it."

"You don't know 'em?"

Something about the marshal's suddenly wily look turned Slocum cautious. He shook his head.

"Might be you got yourself some desperadoes wanted fer a whole passel of crimes." The marshal sat the fancy hand-tooled boots Slocum had taken off one claim-jumper on his desk and admired them. Slocum could almost read the lawman's mind: *These boots'd fit me.*

"They're not doing anyone any good now. Dead men don't need boots," Slocum said. Marshal Borrega jumped again, showing how close Slocum had come to voicing the man's thoughts.

"Look through this here pile of posters and see if you kin identify any of 'em."

Slocum riffled through the inch-thick stack and pulled out three with likenesses close enough to match the men who had tried to murder him in his sleep.

"Could be these three," Slocum said. He quickly read the descriptions and saw all three rode together and were suspected of claim-jumping, although the warrants out for them were for bank robbery in Las Animas.

"You jist earned yerself two hundred dollars," the marshal said. "A hunnerd fer the leader and fifty each fer them fellas." The lawman looked like he sat on an anthill. He shifted and turned and finally stared Slocum squarely in the eye and asked, "This here claim of yers. It proved yet?"

"Why? You think these three might have tried to kill me because there's gold on it?"

"Any land left around that might be, uh, profitable?"

Slocum saw that the marshal had succumbed to gold fever.

"Can't say. You'd have to ask the land agent. What about the reward for those three?" Slocum tapped the wanted posters on the marshal's desk, wondering if his own picture might be on a yellowed sheet farther down the stack.

"I'll send a telegram to the federal marshal in Denver and get the money wired here. Ought to take a week or so." Marshal Borrega licked his lips and ran his fingers over the fancy boots. "What're you going to do with these?"

"The guns I can sell, if they're not evidence. Why don't you keep the boots, Marshal? They look to be about your size." Slocum hoped the marshal was too engrossed in putting on the boots to remember that Slocum had three horses, also. Slocum intended to use them to replace the ones he had bartered away to Bear Tail. With the six-guns and other gear, he stood to make a tidy, if unexpected, profit off the three bushwhackers.

"Good doin' business with ya, Slocum. I'll see to the rewards." Marshal Borrega stared down at his flashy new boots, so recently resting on the feet of a man willing to shoot another while he slept.

Slocum stuffed the guns into the burlap bag and left, whistling to himself. It wouldn't be long before the marshal told everyone in town about the claim-jumpers and that Slocum had something worth stealing. But he had another stop to make before returning to his claim. He stopped in at the general store and sold the six-shooters and the rest of the outlaws' gear, then led the horses to the livery stable. Smitty sat in the shade. The livery stable owner took a long pull at a bottle, corked it and then wiped his lips.

"I do declare, Slocum, you leave with horses, you show up with dif'ernt ones."

"For sale. You have any others for me to peddle?"

"Got one. Gent took a real dislike to payin' fer his horse's hay. Now he's got to worry how to pay the doc fer settin' a busted nose." Smitty rubbed his knuckles against his shirt and smiled.

"I have to talk to the editor of the newspaper. You happen to know his name?"

"The danged editor of the *Winged Victory*? What business you have with a varmint like Micah Underwood? That man never saw a truth he couldn't twist or a lie he couldn't pass off as the truth."

"So you don't much like him," Slocum guessed.

"Wish he'd been the one I'd invited to lunch while I was servin' up my knuckle sandwich," Smitty said. "He said some mighty nasty things about me when he blowed into town a few months back. Said I was chargin' fer services I did not deliver."

Smitty spoke with exaggerated precision, mimicking what the editor of the town paper must have said in an editorial.

"He bad-mouthed durn near every business in this town. Made me wonder why he didn't keep travellin' instead of roostin' here."

"Might be he thought he could improve conditions in Victory," Slocum said. He was taking a shine to Underwood and hadn't even met the man.

"Leave yer danged horses. Be back at twilight to sell them critters, but I'm takin' out the cost of any hay they eat."

Slocum nodded agreement and hurried off. In a town the size of Victory it didn't take him long to find the newspaper office, set off to one end and looking insignificant. Underwood hadn't even bothered putting out a sign telling what business was run from the tumbledown shack, but Slocum knew this was the right place because he heard the mechanical clanking of a Ramage press turning out a new edition.

He entered the front door of the *Winged Victory* and

hesitated. The stifling heat almost pushed him back into the street. The weather had turned cooler, and Slocum had adjusted to it. The printing press and the half-dozen coal oil lamps scattered around the print shop to give a better look at the finished product as it came off the flatbed press caused Slocum to shuck off his jacket.

The man he took to be Micah Underwood hardly looked up from his work.

"You got thirty seconds to tell me why you want the job. You got any experience?"

"Not working at a newspaper," Slocum said, wondering what the editor was talking about. He went to a table and picked up the still-damp edition and glanced at it. A small boxed article at the bottom asked for both a printer's devil and a subscription salesman. Slocum dropped the paper back onto the stack.

"Then why the hell do I want to talk to you?"

"I've got a story that will shake everyone up all the way to Denver. Maybe beyond."

"All my stories are earthshakers. I've got a paper to print. Either help or get out."

Slocum tossed his coat onto a chair and began moving the wet copies to a table where the ink could dry without smearing. He took the papers with set ink and bundled them twenty-five to the stack.

"Anyone else might want to know that the Mother Lode Mine doesn't actually belong to Basil Aiken? That it's on Ute land?"

This stopped Underwood. He froze, then straightened. The next copy of the *Winged Victory* forgotten for the moment on the printer.

"That's mighty provocative."

"Who'd be interested in printing the story, since you aren't? Somebody at the *Rocky Mountain News*?"

"What do those knuckleheads know about the newspaper business? I worked there almost a year and they never impressed me," Underwood said, wiping his hands on a filthy rag. "But you interest me—if the story's on the up-and-up."

"Not asking you to buy a pig in a poke," Slocum said. "I've been out in the mountains for a spell and came across a Ute chief by the name of Bear Tail. He's mighty upset that Aiken is digging in his land, his land granted by treaty with the U.S. Government."

"Ah, the People of the Shining Mountains have always had trouble understanding our need to grub around in the ground for precious minerals. Or even coal and lead. They're a hunting people."

"Do tell," Slocum said dryly.

"Sorry, I didn't realize I was thinking out loud about what to put into an article on the matter. Preaching to the choir in your case, I should imagine." He eyed Slocum more closely and nodded slowly. "You got the look of a man who knows how to talk to the Ute without getting your scalp lifted."

Slocum involuntarily reached up and touched a shock of lank dark hair poking out from under his hat. He had come mighty close to losing his scalp, but not in any of his dealings with Bear Tail. His life, perhaps, but not his scalp.

"Didn't realize they were so close to going on the warpath again," Slocum said. "I thought Chief Ouray had them all calmed down."

"What kind of story are you peddling? Are the Utes upset over the mining or not?"

"The best way to find out is if I take you to Bear Tail and let you talk to him. His English is a little shaky, but you can figure out his concerns."

"You're asking me to ride with you out into the hills?"

"Nope," Slocum said. "I'm asking a reporter to check my facts. If it takes riding bold as brass into a Ute camp, then a real reporter would do it."

"Don't go casting aspersions on either my reporting skills or my bravery, but I have to be sure I'm not going out there to get a bullet in the back. There's more than one ga-loot in this town who doesn't much like me."

"I talked to Smitty at the stables," Slocum said.

"Smitty isn't a violent one, not like that madman who runs the apothecary and puts poison in his medicine."

"Or as Basil Aiken is likely to be if it's true that his mine is on Indian land," Slocum finished. "How many people in town have bought shares in his mine?"

"Every last worthless soul, that's who's bought into his mine," grumbled Underwood. "They'd run me out of town on a rail, after they'd tarred and feathered me, if I showed the Utes were the actual owners of that claim."

"Reckon so," Slocum said, seeing that he had the editor hooked as surely as any cutthroat trout on his line. All he had to do now was reel him in. Gently.

"Why're you doing this? You don't have the look of a good citizen or altruist."

"Don't rightly know what that last means," Slocum said, "and can't remember being called a good citizen anytime in the past few years." It was time to start reeling. "Turns out, my claim might be worth a bit more if Aiken's belongs to somebody else, somebody who doesn't want to dig for gold."

"Like the Utes," finished Underwood, going where Slocum had wanted him to tread. "How far's the Ute camp?"

"Depends on how hard you ride."

"I'll race you there," Micah Underwood said, grinning ear to ear as he grabbed a notebook, a stack of pencils and his coat. The current edition of the *Winged Victory* was forgotten, but Slocum knew there'd be a special edition published when they returned.

"That's a hunting party," Micah Underwood said, almost accusingly.

"That's what the Utes do," Slocum said. "Hunt. This entire stretch of land's theirs by treaty."

"But can this Bear Tail speak for his people? He's not Ouray, after all."

"Not many Utes are happy with their big chief," Slocum said, "but he holds power as much because he can call down the cavalry as muster a thousand warriors from South Park and Middle Park."

"He's a talker, that I'll grant," Underwood said. "I interviewed him a year back, right after the White River Massacre had been settled. He actually made me believe Meeker and his family deserved to be scalped."

"Bear Tail's not that good a talker, but he doesn't have to be."

"Why not?"

"He's got facts—and our law—on his side." Slocum saw that the appeal to facts almost convinced Underwood, and the reporter had yet to talk to Bear Tail.

They rode down the slope slowly and approached the Ute encampment, making no effort to be quiet or hide their presence. Slocum saw a half-dozen braves moving like shadows through the woods and behind boulders. Their number made him a little uneasy since Bear Tail had only that number total in his hunting party. This many sentries meant he was drawing other bands to him and becoming a force to be reckoned with.

"That's him," Slocum said. "The stocky one with the knife in his hand." Slocum tried not to sound too sour about this. Bear Tail held Slocum's old knife. Giving it to the Ute had been right at the time, but Slocum missed the good balance and keen edge. He'd have to scour the stores in Victory and find a new one, or have Smitty make him one since the liveryman had some skills as a blacksmith.

Soon enough, he'd have the money to buy just about anything he wanted.

"Hello, Bear Tail," Slocum called. "I have brought the man who speaks to many. Tell him what you told me about the treaty and your land."

"Come. We smoke. Then we talk."

Slocum had hoped to hurry the Indian along, but Bear Tail operated on a different time scale and nothing would rush him. Slocum and Underwood dismounted and sat by the fire, smoking Bear Tail's pipe until long after sundown. Only then did the Ute launch into his story of stolen land and treaties broken. Underwood dutifully recorded it all, then asked pointed questions.

Slocum was glad to see that Bear Tail was not offended by the reporter's bluntness. He took his time answering, but the results were all Slocum could have wanted. At first Underwood showed a tad of skepticism, but as the night wore on, he became more eager to write down every word Bear Tail uttered.

It was going to be one hell of a special edition of the *Winged Victory*.

# 13

"This is terrible!" Daisy Stevenson stared in horror as the crowd surged down the street, waving fists in the air and more than one carrying axe-handles or pitchforks. The mob had grown uglier by the minute after the *Winged Victory* edition hit the street just after midday. Micah Underwood had worked all night without sleep to get a complete edition out quickly all by himself.

Slocum had known what to expect, but the fury of the prospectors who had been told their claims might not be good was only fuel added to the fire of those who had bought stock in Aiken's Mother Lode Mine. They all saw money—and their very lives—being destroyed in a flash.

"Marshal Borrega had better come out of his burrow and do something," Slocum said. He doubted the marshal would budge. If anything, he might join the crowd since Slocum suspected that the lawman had sunk a fair amount of money into stock certificates for Aiken's mine and that the money might not have come from his own pocket. The city of Victory needed to audit its books to see if Borrega had dipped into that shallow pond to wet his beak illegally.

"Who are they going after?" Daisy asked, looking more puzzled than worried now. "They might be going to the newspaper office to lynch Underwood."

Slocum thought she would prefer that to the alternative, but the crowd had stopped in front of the office Aiken had rented and had made such a production out of opening to any investor in the Mother Lode Mine.

"Where's your brother?"

"I . . . I don't k-know," Daisy said, the stutter coming into her voice to betray her uneasiness. "H-he wasn't back at the cabin last n-night. I'd hoped you would show up, so I d-didn't go looking for Andy."

"I was out at my claim."

"You have a claim?" Daisy's eyebrows rose. "And here you were the one pooh-poohing the idea of gold being found."

"Apparently it's here but on Ute land," Slocum said. "That's what the paper reported." Underwood had faithfully reported every word Bear Tail had uttered, adding only enough to make the Ute sound as if he had graduated from Harvard. With Bear Tail declaring the land under and around the Mother Lode Mine as sacred Ute country, Aiken had few options left. Or so Slocum hoped.

"There's Andy!" she called. "Andy!" The young man was trapped between the locked door leading into Aiken's office and the crowd. Slocum took in the situation and knew Stevenson was not likely to walk away from this unscathed. The crowd's anger was too great and the shouting, cursing men needed to vent their spleen some way. Tearing Stevenson apart would not sate that fury but would only fuel it.

"Stay here," Slocum said. "Don't move."

"But, John—" Daisy spoke to empty air. Slocum ducked into the Sweetwater Saloon and ran for the stairs leading up to the cribs. None of the prostitutes were in their tiny rooms. They were milling around the edge of the crowd, probably as mad as any of the men since many of them had been paid for their services with stock certificates.

Slocum ducked into one room, then hurried to the next and the next until he found one shoulder-wide room with a window. He jumped over the tattered mattress on the floor and threw open the window. Slocum got his feet braced against the windowsill, then shot out like a pouncing cougar. Flying across the gap between the saloon and the building next to it, Slocum stretched out. His fingers barely caught the edge of the distant roof. He slammed hard against the splintery side, then began struggling to pull himself up. Slocum kicked and scrabbled and finally tumbled to the roof.

Panting, he made his way to the front. Below him stretched the angry crowd with Andrew Stevenson caught between locked door and boiling anger. Sucking in a deep breath, Slocum stepped off the roof and dropped two stories to land hard amid the leaders of the crowd. Several were knocked over but hardly anyone else paid any attention. Slocum stood, shoved back another man and established himself as a bulwark for Stevenson against the crowd.

"I've got something you want to hear," Slocum shouted. His words were drowned by the irate cries. "Listen to me!" When it became obvious no one was going to obey him, Slocum slipped his six-shooter from its holster and fired into the air. The first shot did nothing, but the second caused a deathly quiet to drop over the crowd.

"Listen to me," Slocum shouted. "I want to—"

He never got any further. The door clicked and clacked as the locking bar inside was pulled back. Stepping out, Basil Aiken looked as if nothing had happened.

"My fellow citizens, I want to talk to you!" Aiken's voice carried clarion-crisp and rang with confidence, but it reignited the crowd's wrath.

"We're going to string you up, you fraud! You sold us stock certificates for a mine on Indian land!"

"Worthless stock!" yelled another.

"Lynch him!" shouted a miner at the rear of the throng. The crowd pushed forward again, grumbling about the best way to mete out their version of justice. Someone called out, "Necktie party!"

Slocum saw that Andy Stevenson simply stood as if in shock. He didn't appear to understand what angered the crowd or that he was likely to be the focus for it by selling everyone with two nickels to rub together the bogus stock. Slocum fired his six-gun again. A small cascade of wood and dust rained down, but only Stevenson noticed it. This more than anything else galvanized the young man to move away, slipping along the wall and following his sister's impassioned cries for him to join her at the Sweetwater Saloon next door.

"What you gonna do, Aiken? You gonna give us back our money? You swindled us. That mine's on Indian land!"

"I'm as much at a loss as any of you," Aiken said. Seeing that the crowd didn't care if he left town wearing only his fancy shoes, he changed his tack. "I was taken by surprise when I read Mr. Underwood's editorial. Are we sure he has his facts right? I'm not. He has a reputation for scurrilous, lying attacks, doesn't he? Maybe he's just stirring the pot until it boils."

Aiken appeared proud of himself diverting the crowd's wrath to the unpopular newspaper editor. But the tactic worked for only a few seconds.

"How come you didn't ask first if them Utes owned the land?"

"It is public land," Aiken said, but again he saw this argument wasn't working. "We can dicker with the tribe. They will surrender their claim to the land for enough trade goods. What do they care for gold?"

"They won't trade," Slocum said. "That's sacred land to them. Might even be a burial ground." He had no idea if this was true, but there had been a lull between Aiken's statement and the crowd's response. This was as good a chance as he'd get to advance his plan.

"Everyone has a price," Aiken said confidently. "I will speak with these savages and convince them to make way for progress."

"Who knows if there's even gold up there? All we seen was a couple nuggets your man Touhy brought back." The crowd began to mutter and turn ugly again.

More angry calls for Aiken to be lynched.

For two cents Slocum would have let the crowd have its way, as distasteful as lynchings were to him. But if Aiken got his neck stretched, Daisy and her brother would never get their money back. Along with most of Victory, they'd end up broke. The only winners would be Aiken's wife in Denver and all the mistresses he had accumulated across Colorado as they tapped into the bank accounts he had set up for them. And the money in the one Daisy had established would go untouched, since Aiken was undoubtedly the only shareholder in Consolidated Shipping.

"I've got a good gold claim, and it's not on Indian land," Slocum said loudly. For a few seconds the crowd continued to make catcalls and lewd suggestions, then these died and all eyes fixed on Slocum. He felt Aiken's hot gaze spear him like he was a piece of rare steak on a hungry man's platter.

"What's this you're saying, Mr. Slocum?"

"Might be more gold than in the Mother Lode Mine," Slocum said truthfully.

"More?"

"I've got to get an assay done, but Mr. Aiken here's an expert on ore and its gold content. Might be he could look over my claim and see what he thinks of it." Slocum locked eyes with Aiken in a battle of wills. Aiken knew he was lying but was caught in the net of deception he had already cast over the citizens of Victory.

"While I deal with the Utes over this unfortunate, undoubtedly trivial land ownership issue, I'll do as Mr. Slocum suggests and see what might be on his claim."

"Anybody who wants to come, saddle up and let's ride," Slocum called. He saw Aiken turn paler by several shades. "You need a horse, Mr. Aiken? I'll ask Smitty over at the stables to fix you up."

"I, uh, I have a horse."

"Everyone who wants to come along and see what Mr. Aiken thinks of my claim, follow me!" Slocum waved his arm and hurried to get his horse. This was going to be quite a sideshow.

"Well, Aiken, whatya think? Does Slocum have a decent claim or not?" The old prospector peered at Aiken, who turned over a rock in his hands, studying it from every angle.

"There's more like this?" Aiken asked.

"Whole pile over yonder," Slocum said, pointing. There was a rush from a dozen men who had come from town to pick up the rocks and examine them.

"Lordy, this here's a vein of gold runnin' smack through the whole danged mountain!" cried one man. Slocum recognized him as the owner of the town bakery. Another snatched the rock from the baker's grip and held it up to catch the light.

"Don't know. Might be fool's gold."

"Might be, but it's not," said Aiken. "This is one of the richest claims I have ever seen. It might well be the richest ever found in the whole state of Colorado."

"What you gonna do about the Mother Lode Mine?"

"I've dispatched my associate to speak with the Ute chief, this Bear Tail, the one who gave Micah Underwood such a stirring tale of, uh, burial on that land and how the Great White Father in Washington supposedly allows them to use it forever and ever."

"What's that mean?"

"I'm going to take care of it. But until the Mother Lode

Mine title is free and clear of all encumbrances, we should take heart in Mr. Slocum's fine discovery. This only repeats everything I've said so far. This is gold country, and there're fortunes to be made."

Basil Aiken turned a little paler when the men pawing through the cairn of stones Slocum had put out began whispering, a few trying to hide the smaller rocks with gold trace and steal them for themselves.

"Looks like these gents know gold when they see it, and this isn't the right kind of quartz for fool's gold," Slocum said.

"He's right on that score," the old prospector said. "I seen my share of fool's gold. This is the real McCoy."

"It looks as if you're a rich man, Slocum." Aiken looked around, as if wanting to escape.

"I'd say I was a lucky one, about as lucky as you, Mr. Aiken, finding gold so quick and easy."

"What's that?"

"Not just anyone can wander around these mountains and find rock with gold in it like me and you," said Slocum.

"I have to admit that is so."

"What're you doin' 'bout the Mother Lode Mine? Who's out palaverin' with them Injuns?" demanded the prospector. "I got me nigh on a hunnerd dollars worth of stock in yer mine."

This caused the others to begin muttering about losing everything if the Mother Lode actually belonged to the Utes. Aiken looked as if he would lose his breakfast at any instant.

"Really a shame, too," Slocum said. He looked squarely at Aiken as he spoke.

"About the Mother Lode Mine?"

"No, sir, about me having no real interest in proving this claim. I happened on the land, it looked right, and I registered it with the land office. But spending the long hours getting rich pulling gold by the buckets from the claim, that's not for me."

"You're selling?" asked Aiken, a quaver in his voice. Realization came slowly to him what Slocum was saying.

"You're sellin'?" piped up the prospector. "If 'n I hadn't wasted so danged much of my stake, I'd buy this one. It's rich, rich!"

"I'd sell for a thousand dollars and be on my way," Slocum said.

"A thousand?" Aiken swallowed hard.

"A smart man could cut up the property and make that much reselling it."

"I don't know. That's a powerful lot, but I'm willing to buy from you," Aiken hurried on when he read the expressions of the men from town.

"If you bought it, would that make it part of the Mother Lode Mine claim?"

"You mean, if Aiken here buys your claim, it'd also be ours? Part ours 'cuz we done bought stock in the Mother Lode?"

"It would look that way to me," Slocum said, stoking the fires a bit higher.

"I'll buy your claim, Slocum. Will you take my check? It's good, I assure you."

"I prefer cash," Slocum said. "Hell, I'd prefer gold dust, but I'll take greenbacks."

They dickered for a few more minutes and Aiken eventually drew out his wallet and disgorged almost a thousand dollars, handing it reluctantly to Slocum.

"There, Slocum. This claim's mine now."

"All signed, sealed and witnessed," Slocum said, signing his name to the transfer deed with a flourish. "The fine citizens of Victory are all witnesses."

"We surely are," piped up the baker. "And we're witnesses that this is part of the Mother Lode Mine, too. If the original mine belongs to the Indians, then this one'll make us all rich!"

A cheer went up.

"Looks like I pulled your fat out of the fire," Slocum said softly to Aiken.

"You've got a wad of my money, Slocum."

"Nice we could do business since we're so much alike."

"We're *nothing* alike, Slocum. Nothing!"

"I wouldn't say that, Aiken." Slocum reached into his pocket and tossed the man the shotgun shell he had picked up at the salted Mother Lode Mine. "I'd say we're more alike than either of us wants to mention."

Aiken crushed the shell in his grip, then stuffed it into his pocket as he glared at Slocum.

"My money's not all you've got, Slocum."

"If you're saying I've got brass balls, thanks for the compliment."

"I'm saying," Aiken said with cold menace, "you've got my money—and my rancor. You'd better ride soon and you'd better ride fast."

# 14

"It's so ironic, isn't it John, that you were the one who said there wasn't any gold here and now you're rich? Imagine Mr. Aiken paying so much for your claim!" Daisy Stevenson heaved a deep sigh. Slocum watched in appreciation as her breasts rose and fell, but the slight flush to the woman's cheeks showed the real beauty. Never had Daisy looked more radiant. The brisk autumn wind blowing from the direction of what had been his staked-out claim pulled her blond hair back and rustled it in a banner, but her face was nothing less than glowing.

It might have been the promise of winter's bite to the freezing air or the thought of so much money that gave her this charm. Slocum didn't much care at the moment.

"He bought more than my claim," Slocum said.

"What else?" she asked.

"He bought a shotgun shell, too."

"What do you mean? I don't understand. What shotgun shell?"

Slocum shook his head. He didn't want to explain to her the game he played and how he had forced Aiken to buy another plot of worthless land. The more he added to the mining magnate's expenses, the more likely Aiken was to give up swindling the people of Victory and move on. He might not repay the people of Victory for the bogus stock certificates he had sold them but he wouldn't fleece them anymore.

"It's complicated. Let's just say I know how much gold is at my old claim—and so does Aiken."

"Of course he does. He's a mining engineer, an expert," Daisy said. "Sometimes, John, you talk in riddles."

"Then I'm going to be as plain as that pretty little nose on your face. You and your brother should get out of town right now. Leave. Go back to Denver. Go West. Go to Mexico. It doesn't matter. Just leave Victory."

"Why? You're proof that there's money to be gained here. We can't leave when we're so close. You even helped us out, finding that claim of yours. Since it is part of the Mother Lode Mine any gold found in the Slocum Mine is going to make us rich that much faster."

"Aiken isn't going to clear up the mess with the Mother Lode Mine, and there's no gold on my claim. He knows it and so do I."

"Oh, you're joshing me again, aren't you, John? It's so hard to tell sometimes. Mr. Aiken wouldn't have bought your claim if there hadn't been a lot of gold there. He's no fool."

"He's no fool," Slocum agreed, but arguing with such determined greed on Daisy's part again proved to be completely foolish.

"There's supposed to be an announcement at noon today. Will you come with me?" She looked at him with her sparkling eyes, and any thought Slocum might have had of moving on and leaving her and her brother to their fate vanished.

"What's happening?"

"I don't know, but Mr. Aiken said it was a big announcement and he wanted everyone in town there."

Slocum held out his arm for Daisy to take, then they

made their way slowly down the boardwalk. The demeanor of the townspeople had improved a little after Slocum had sold his holdings to Aiken, but an undercurrent of tension still made it feel as if a single misstep would ignite the crowd and release its full wrath.

"On stage again," Slocum said, shaking his head in wonder. Aiken loved the dramatic and needed it now to regain the upper hand over the local citizens. Aiken and Touhy stood shoulder to shoulder, whispering to avoid being overheard. Whatever Touhy told Aiken, it wasn't well-received. The mining magnate visibly forced himself to keep down an eruption of anger. If Slocum had to bet, Touhy had been sent to dicker with Bear Tail over the fate of the Mother Lode Mine and had returned with no deal.

Touhy had probably offered blankets or tins of food. Slocum had promised Bear Tail more horses. The Utes, like most other tribes, valued animals above all else, especially things they saw as inferior white man's goods. Slocum understood the situation far better than Touhy—or Aiken—ever could.

The people gathered at the base of the stage but unlike before there were no spontaneous cheers. If anything, Slocum had the feeling this was more like the crowd that would show up at a funeral. Nobody talked or even looked at the man on either side of him. What noise there was came from the saloons where many had not bothered leaving their warm beers to hear what Aiken might say. In the span of a few short days, Aiken's fame had taken a big hit. And his fortune was similarly going to decline, if Slocum had anything to do about it.

"Ladies and gentlemen!" called Aiken in his booming voice. "There have been great changes the past day or two." He did not pause to let the mumbling build into full-fledged opposition. The last thing Aiken dared do was let someone in the crowd ask for his money back. "More gold has been discovered, this time on new property bought by the Mother Lode Mining Company. We've got an uncontested mine to exploit!"

This settled some in the crowd, but Slocum wanted to shout out that he had salted the claim, just as Aiken had salted the Mother Lode. But Daisy was beside herself with excitement, and Slocum didn't want to rain on her parade. Not that it would do him any good. She was completely devoted to the notion that Basil Aiken was going to make her and Andy rich.

"My able assistant, Mr. Andrew Stevenson, has continued his unceasing effort to bring you all the opportunity to share in our bounty. He has sold all the shares that have come available through our purchases. It is my great pleasure to award Andy with his second gold bullet."

Daisy cheered and clapped wildly. Others nearby also applauded but with more restraint.

"Here, son, here is an unprecedented *second* gold bullet to commemorate your hard work." Aiken held the gleaming bullet high and let the sun catch it. Slocum was the only one who noticed that a storm cloud crossed the sun as Aiken held the bullet above his head so the golden gleam vanished and an ominous shadow was cast across the crowd.

Stevenson took the bullet, fished out the other one Aiken had given him and displayed both. This time the sight of the gold spurred the crowd to more a more enthusiastic response. Aiken shook his hand and launched into a new sales pitch, insisting the stock certificates being sold were not only valid but also everyone's road to riches.

Stevenson let his boss continue his harangue and jumped down, eager to show his sister his new award.

"I'm the first one to ever get a second gold bullet," Stevenson said proudly. "Imagine that, Sis. And if I work even harder, we'll still get rich. We've just got to."

"How much have you loaned Aiken?" asked Slocum.

"Loaned him? Why, nothing," Stevenson said, frowning. "I don't see what you're getting at, Mr. Slocum."

"We've been paid back in stock certificates," Daisy said.

"Three hundred dollars? Is that a fair number? I'll give you four hundred if you pack up and leave."

"Go where?" Andy Stevenson looked confused.

"Anywhere," Slocum said. "Aiken is using you and you'll be left holding the bag."

"Now, John, we've been over this, you and I. We're not budging. There's gold to be mined. The next time I go to Denver, it'll be with a suitcase full of our money."

"What's that?" Stevenson looked at his sister. "I don't understand what you mean."

"Nothing, Andy. Just keep working, and I'll do the same. Together, we'll be rich. Really rich because we're willing to work for it," Daisy said with just a hint of contempt in her voice for Slocum's willingness to sell his claim so cheaply.

"Ah, Miss Stevenson," said Aiken, coming up. He struck a pose, thumbs hooked into his suspenders. "Just the lady I was looking for." The man moved in such a way that he interposed himself between Daisy and Slocum. "I need some assistance in the office. Would you be willing to help out?"

"Why, of course, but I was going to help Andy sell more shares of stock."

"He's doing such a fine job, he won't need your help—and I do. The paperwork is flooding in now that we're so close to setting up mining, smelting, transport and all the other businesses required to turn Victory into the biggest town in Colorado!"

"I'll be glad to help," Daisy said, pointedly looking around Aiken at Slocum.

"Ah, yes, Slocum," Aiken said, as if seeing him for the first time. "I thought you'd have drifted on by now."

"I decided to stick around awhile longer," Slocum said. "Who knows? I might even prove another gold mine."

"Yes, there is gold in them thar hills, as they say," Aiken

said. His voice took on an edge as he added, "Up in those dangerous hills. You'd be well advised to watch your step."

"I'll watch my back," Slocum said, not budging an inch in the face of Aiken's threats.

"To work, everyone," Aiken said, hurrying off in the direction of the Mother Lode Mine office.

Before Daisy could follow, Slocum grabbed her arm and held her firmly.

"You're walking into a snake pit," he said.

"John, really!"

"Here, take this," he said, fishing out the derringer he carried in his vest pocket.

"Why would I take that?" Daisy asked, her eyes wide at the sight of the two-shot pistol.

"To make me feel better about you working in Aiken's office," Slocum said. "Don't forget what happened in Denver."

"Denver? What's he talking about, Sis?"

"Oh, Andy, he's only joshing," she said. Daisy hastily took the derringer and tucked it into her small purse to keep her brother from asking more questions she did not want to answer. She nodded curtly at Slocum, then looped her arm through Andy's and said, "We need to get to work, both of us. Go on, sell those stock certificates and I'll take care of the paperwork in the office."

Slocum felt as if he were watching two people walking to the gallows to be hanged. Daisy might discount what had happened in Denver but he couldn't.

The crowd had dispersed, the townspeople going about their business. Slocum couldn't help but compare this with the way they had reacted after Aiken's previous gold bullet presentation. He needed to take a few more horses to Bear Tail to keep up the Ute's insistence that the Mother Lode Mine was on tribal property. That Aiken hadn't sent telegrams to Denver, to the Indian agent, to anyone and everyone demanding a resurvey told him the mining magnate didn't want to rock the boat. He wanted nothing more than to bilk the people of Victory of their money and then move on fast.

"Move on fast," Slocum muttered. That'd be good advice for him to take, but he suspected Basil Aiken would be gone before he was. Turning up his collar to the increasingly bitter wind, he hiked down the street to the *Winged Victory* office. Slocum wasn't sure what it would take for Daisy to see Aiken for what he was, but evidence could turn the rest of the town against the mining magnate. They were already halfway there after the fiasco over having the bulk of their money pulled out from under them by a faulty survey.

Slocum slowed as this thought hit him. He'd have to be careful or Aiken would turn the loss of the Mother Lode Mine against him since he had scouted the area with Andrew Stevenson. Worse than being the scapegoat, Slocum knew Stevenson could also be tarred. This might convince Daisy that Aiken wasn't the hero she thought, but the consequences could be deadly.

"Slocum, there you are!" Micah Underwood waved at Slocum and came hurrying over, the wind whipping at his thin cloth coat. The editor took no notice of the cold as he waved a sheaf of papers in the air. "Got something to show you."

"Something good?" Slocum hoped the editor had found the evidence needed to call in a federal marshal to haul Aiken off to jail.

"Of course it's good. What do you think? That I'd waste your time—and mine?"

"Let's get out of the wind. There's a storm coming."

"There is?" Underwood looked up, adjusted his glasses and caught the wind full in the face, as if noticing it for the first time. "All right, you cracker-assed tenderfoot. Into my office, if you can't stand a little weather."

Slocum shook his head as he followed the editor to his

office. The heat inside was overpowering after the cold outside. Underwood burned lamps all over his office to make sure he could clearly see every line of his newspaper as it came off the flatbed press.

Without being invited, Slocum pulled up a chair and sank into it.

"Look at this. I got proof Aiken's movin' as much money as he can from Victory to accounts in some Denver bank. I can't find out which one, but if I do, this whole story busts wide-open." Underwood shoved the papers he had waved around outside across the table for Slocum to look at. Slocum didn't bother.

"So ? Daisy Stevenson took a suitcase of money to Denver and deposited it in a company account."

"What account?" For once Underwood looked stunned that Slocum knew more than he did.

"Something called Consolidated Shipping."

"She willing to put that on the record so I can print it? I can taste it, nailing this connivin' bastard," Underwood said with glee.

"Miss Stevenson doesn't think she was doing anything wrong."

"Of course she doesn't. That's the way Aiken operates, getting dupes to do what he'd be sent to jail for doing. What else? There's more. I hear it in your voice." Underwood looked at him shrewdly, but Slocum shook his head. He didn't want Aiken knowing what had gone wrong in Denver, although the telegram from Randall probably let him figure out why Daisy hadn't been killed. Slocum still worried that there was more to Randall's attempt on Daisy's life that needed explaining.

"She doesn't know or want to believe she's mixed up in anything illegal," Slocum said. "That's why Aiken tried to kill her in Denver." Slocum took a deep breath when Underwood grabbed his notebook and pencil, licked the lead and then began scribbling.

"Well, go on, man. Who tried to kill her? Do you know? It wasn't Aiken because he never left Victory. Besides, he's not the kind to do his own dirty work."

Slocum had let his thoughts slip past his lips and now regretted it. But Underwood was clever and might throw some light on what had happened, since Slocum was unable to go any farther in figuring it out.

"Aiken's henchman Randall was responsible. We shot it out but I didn't kill him, only scared him off."

"After she came out of the bank?" asked Underwood. "That meant Aiken wanted all witnesses removed. Let Miss Stevenson set up the account and put the money into it, then kill her so it looked like some robbery gone wrong."

Slocum blinked. He had been looking at the attempted murder from the wrong perspective. He remembered how Daisy had set down the suitcase with the money where no one in the street could see it—where it was hidden from Randall. She had lived in Denver and knew the streets. She had arrived at the bank before Randall.

"I think Randall jumped the gun and thought Daisy had already deposited the money and was coming *out* of the bank," said Slocum. "Either that or he wanted the money for himself. He could steal a suitcase filled with Aiken's hard-swindled cash and have the entire distance across Colorado as a head start."

"That kind of money would go a long way toward starting a new life 'bout anywhere out West," Underwood said, still writing as he talked.

Slocum snorted contemptuously. "A man like Randall would whore and drink and gamble it away in a month or two. If somebody didn't rob him of it when he got to bragging on how smart he was. It seems more likely he mistakenly thought Daisy had finished her chores in the bank and that it was all right to kill her—as Aiken ordered. Randall is Aiken's man, through and through."

"This fits in well with what I think is going on. Aiken is sending money to Denver but it never is deposited in the Mother Lode Mining Company account. It all goes in the account Miss Stevenson established. He's sucking this town dry like a juicy peach." Underwood looked up from his scribbling and smiled. "Now, you gonna tell me what really happened out there?"

"In Denver? That's about it." Slocum grew wary. Underwood was probing in places where Slocum knew danger lay.

"With the Utes and that claim they own the land where Aiken stuck up his sign saying: GOLD HERE. I haven't been around these parts long but nobody'd ever whispered that was treaty land. You looked mighty cozy with Bear Tail, if I say so."

"It's your newspaper. You can say what you please, but keep it in the editorial, not as a news story."

"You're a cagey fellow, Slocum. I don't like that in politicians but those who flummox politicians—and crooked mine owners—that's a different kettle of fish."

"Glad you approve," Slocum said dryly.

Underwood laughed.

"We got a lot in common, you and me, Slocum."

"Mostly in our desire to see that Aiken gets what he deserves," Slocum said.

"That, too. Now this Randall fellow, is he the one with Touhy and Zach Hubbell who—"

"Hubbell? Is that Zach's last name? Nobody seemed to know when I asked around."

"He's a slippery one. I can understand why you didn't hear anyone mention his full name. Real backshooter. Getting a line on him was almost as hard as tickling a trout. I suspect he's got a reward on his head—I'm not a gambling man, but I'd give odds that there's a warrant issued for him." Underwood canted his head to one side as he studied Slocum's reaction. "You're more likely to collect it than for those three claim-jumpers. The marshal's got that money all spent 'fore it even arrives."

"Let him keep the money. I got plenty when I sold off their belongings," said Slocum.

"Except for the boots."

Slocum studied Micah Underwood with new appreciation. There wasn't much of anything that went on in Victory that escaped his keen gaze. He had not thought there was much hope of ever bringing Aiken to justice, short of a lynching or a bullet, but Slocum was changing his mind. Underwood was tenacious and loved to keep the pot boiling. There might be hope.

"Getting back to the story," Underwood pressed on, "you willing to state that Randall tried to kill Miss Stevenson? If we can tie him in with Aiken, this might be all that I'd need for a couple really hard-hitting articles."

"I'm as sure it was him as I can be, but he's back in Denver. Finding him in that rat's nest would be nigh on impossible."

Underwood laughed.

"You need to ask around more, Slocum. Randall's back in town. Came in this morning, just before Aiken's gold bullet ceremony. You didn't see him because he's supposed to be lying low."

Slocum touched the six-shooter in his holster and nodded. He would have ventilated Randall if he had spotted him anywhere near Daisy.

"Where is he? Or didn't your source of information know?"

"Give me credit for knowing my job, Slocum. Of course I know where he is. There's a spare room at the rear of Aiken's fancy office. Can't hardly see the door because it's hidden in the unlit part of the room, but it's there—and it leads directly to our Mr. Randall. Want to go ask him a few questions?"

"Lead the way," Slocum said. He didn't cotton much to

going back into the cold wind and facing the storm brewing over the mountains, but inside the print shop was a mite too stuffy for him. Underwood grabbed a coat with voluminous pockets and stuffed his notebook into the right front. With a quick, practiced gesture, he rested his pencil over his ear and went to the door.

"This is the part of the job that's the most fun," Underwood said.

He opened the door and two loud reports rang out. Underwood staggered back, clutching his chest. He looked down at the blood oozing between his fingers, then stared at Slocum as he fell to the floor, dead.

# 15

Slocum's hand flashed to his six-shooter and drew, aiming at the empty space above Micah Underwood's body. It had passed twilight outside and this section of town was inky black. The gaslights along the main street hissed and popped. But since many had not been properly lit, they cast only a shimmering, shaky yellow light that hid more than it revealed. Slocum slipped out of the *Winged Victory* office and pressed his back against the wall. He turned slowly one way and the other, hunting for the owlhoot who had gunned down the editor so ruthlessly.

The wind whined but other than a few off-key songs sung boisterously a block away in a saloon he heard nothing. Then came the crunch of boots and two men appeared out of shadow.

"Why'd you kill him, Slocum? Why'd you murder Micah like that?" Accusing him was Basil Aiken and at his side, head bobbing up and down, stood Touhy. Touhy held a rifle and pointed it in Slocum's general direction.

"He raises that long gun another inch and he's dead," Slocum warned.

"That's what we'd expect from a man who gunned down the town's most honest man," Aiken said. "Other than myself, of course. You're a criminal, Slocum. A murderer. We have to take you in. Don't make us get a posse."

More steps, running this time. A man out of breath. Popping from the shadows as suddenly as Aiken and Touhy had, Marshal Borrega waved his six-gun around.

"Marshal, you've come just in time to arrest Slocum. Take him away. He murdered Micah Underwood." Aiken struck a pose like an orator and pointed his pudgy finger dramatically. Slocum would have laughed if the situation hadn't been so serious. His hand tensed around the ebony butt of his six-shooter. If he landed in the town jail, it wouldn't be long before Aiken whipped up enough sentiment among all his stockholders to bring a raging lynch mob to take justice into its own hands. The way people grumbled all the time now in Victory, after learning the Mother Lode Mine was on Ute land, venting a little bile with a necktie party would be seen as perfectly acceptable. No one had much cared for Underwood or his crusading ways, but that would be forgotten as soon as the rope was knotted into a neck-breaking noose.

A noose that would fit Slocum perfectly.

"What are you goin' on about, Mr. Aiken? Slocum didn't murder nobody. Not here, at any rate," Borrega said. "I was comin' over to palaver with Underwood when I seen him comin' out. A bushwhacker stepped out of the shadow, 'bout where you're standin' now, Mr. Aiken, and shot Underwood."

"You're not accusing me of murder, are you, Marshal? That would be a terrible mistake, I assure you."

"Ain't sayin' you had spit to do with it, Mr. Aiken. Fact is, I know you didn't."

This startled Slocum. He thought the marshal was building up to arresting Aiken.

"You think I'm always outta breath? I chased the varmint to the edge of town, but he got away. Had a horse waitin' fer him."

"Did you see who it was, Marshal?" asked Slocum.

"Too dark, and he had his back to me the whole time. From what he was wearin', hell, he coulda been anyone in town. Can't even guess how tall he was. But he lit out for the high country."

"There's a storm coming fast," Slocum said. "If we want to catch him, we've got to get on the trail right now, Marshal."

"Reckon so," Borrega said with resignation. He obviously preferred breaking up fights in saloons and knocking back drinks he got in return from barkeeps. But he was enough of a lawman to know he had to keep the murders to a minimum in town, especially when they were so cold-blooded—and of prominent citizens.

"There's no need, Marshal," protested Aiken. "Slocum did it. I . . ."

"Are you sayin' you saw the killin'? Where was you hidin'? I came along the street and saw it as good as anybody could. Slocum was inside and the killer was out here in the street."

Borrega turned suddenly and grabbed, snatching Slocum's pistol from his hand with a snakelike movement. The marshal sniffed the muzzle, then tossed the Colt back. "Ain't been fired. Not recently, at any rate. Now, you want to join the posse, Mr. Aiken? How about you, Touhy? Didn't think so."

He hitched up his drawers and said to Slocum, "I'll round up whoever I kin. If you can track him, we'll run the varmint to the ground in two shakes of a lamb's tail."

Aiken and Touhy muttered angrily, with Touhy finally subsiding. Slocum eyed them for a moment, then went to saddle his horse. Things moved quickly—too quickly for Micah Underwood. With any luck, they might run down the killer Borrega so luckily saw escaping.

Slocum saddled his roan and waited anxiously for the marshal and the rest of the posse. His heart sank when he saw Borrega had found only three others. Then he sat a mite straighter. It'd be better with only a handful of them. They could ride faster and not have to cater to the men only along for the money. Too often hangers-on rode with a posse figuring someone else would do the shooting and arresting so they could divvy up the reward for nothing more than being there. This way, with so few deputies, everyone knew the risk of shooting it out when they cornered the killer.

With more determination, Slocum followed the marshal to the edge of town where the lawman claimed to have lost the fleeing owlhoot. Slocum dropped to the ground, read the tracks and saw how Borrega had chased Underwood's killer. And as the marshal said, a set of fresh tracks led off into the night. The spitting rain all day helped turn the ground soft. The tracks were sharp, clear and so obvious a blind man could follow. Slocum led the posse up into the mountains where the ground turned rockier and tracking in the dark was proving to be more difficult by the minute.

"Hold up, Slocum," Borrega said when they came to a junction in the trail.

"Not giving up, are you, Marshal?"

"You're havin' a mighty hard time findin' any trace now, ain't you?"

"I—"

"Hold your horses, man. I know this country. A little bit. I'm jist pointin' out how hard it is for you to work. If we split up, half the posse to the right and the rest along this here trail, we stand a better chance of runnin' him to ground. The two canyons meet up five, six miles from here in a broad valley."

Slocum looked at the three deputies, now nervous as brides. Five men riding together might give a bigger target; it also provided five guns to shoot back. Dividing the posse meant more of a chance of being attacked from ambush.

"You're right, Marshal. How're you going to split us up?"

"These three young men can take that trail," Borrega said, pointing to the right. "It's got a better path through it to Green Valley. Me and you kin take this one."

Slocum had a gut feeling this was the one taken by the fleeing killer. He wondered if Borrega had a similar instinct or if he just wanted to ride with Slocum.

The ugly thought came to Slocum that Borrega might be helping the killer, and this was a good way to eliminate a thorn in Aiken's side. They'd ride along, the killer would be waiting and Slocum would be caught in a deadly cross fire, from the killer's gun and Borrega's at his back. Aiken had the money to arrange such a thing, and hadn't Borrega already hinted broadly at how he wanted a cut of the action on the gold mining?

Slocum pushed the notion aside. He doubted Borrega was that clever or subtle. And all the marshal had needed to do if he wanted Slocum out of the way was to agree with Aiken and Touhy. Slocum would have spent the night in jail and from the next morning on through eternity with a rope around his broken neck.

"Think they can do all right on their own?" Slocum asked, watching the other three in the posse ride away fearfully.

"This is the right track, ain't it? I'm not as good as you but even I kin see it."

"So they'll be at the far end of this canyon, where it leads into the valley, waiting for the killer, if we flush him?"

"And if we don't flush 'im, we'll shoot him." Marshal Borrega made it sound simple.

"We'd better get a move on," Slocum said, looking up into the sky. What stars there had been were all gone now, hidden beneath a thick layer of storm clouds. The wind was picking up and carried the knife-edge of winter with it. Slocum inhaled deeply and shuddered. There might be more than a flurry of snow, too, since it smelled about right for an early blizzard.

"Best to let the others get a head start so they'll actually be at the valley waitin'. Theirs is a lot shorter path than ours. This here canyon winds around 'fore it straightens out and runs smack into Green Valley."

Slocum pulled his coat closer, wishing he had something heavier. He might get out his duster and wear it over the coat but it wasn't that cold. Yet.

What light there had been was gone now behind the thick, roiling clouds, but occasional bolts of lightning gave Slocum plenty to see the trail. The fugitive made no effort to hide his tracks. If they dallied long enough, his hoof-prints would be under snow—or on top of a newly fallen layer.

After thirty minutes of riding, Slocum slowed and then dismounted. He flopped belly-down on the dirt and ran his fingers over the tracks. The wind had eroded the sharper portion of the track, but something worried him.

"These might not be the killer's tracks," Slocum said.

"What are you sayin', Slocum?"

"They're older. Might be hours older. Someone else rode this way."

"Could be on their way to Green Valley. There's more 'n one ranch up there and cattle stray this direction."

"The prints are going to the valley and I don't see any sign of cattle."

Marshal Borrega shrugged.

"Jist one of them things. This here part of the country's been overrun with prospectors huntin' fer gold."

Slocum mounted, unsure of the marshal's line of thought. The old tracks were from a horse, not a mule, and the horse had been trotting along. A prospector might take his time looking around for traces of blue dirt.

"Slocum, there!" cried the marshal. "Ahead. I see a fire. We done run him to ground!"

"Hold on," Slocum urged. He mounted and stood in the stirrups, taking a look at what Borrega had already seen. A small fire, guttering in the wind, had been built not a hundred yards ahead. The wan light from the fire refused to give up any sign of the man cooking over it or using it to keep his hands warm.

"Split up. I'll ride on a ways and you come up on him from this way. We kin catch the owlhoot in a cross fire, if he tries to put up a fuss."

Slocum pulled his Winchester from its sheath and used his knees to guide his horse off the path and into the sparse undergrowth. Borrega made his way along the path until he disappeared in the dark. Slocum heard the *clop-clop* of the marshal's horse until the whine of rising wind drowned it out. He hoped the man at the fire was sleeping. Otherwise, he would be awake and ready to put up a fight to keep from being taken back to Victory for trial.

Finding a decent spot, Slocum dismounted, tethered his horse and advanced on foot, weaving between waist-high rocks until he got to a spot where he could see the small clearing. The fire had burned down to embers by this time, giving Slocum with his dark-adapted eyes a chance to look around. Not five feet upslope from the fire stretched a dark form about the right size of a man lying down with a blanket around him. Slocum continued studying the area for sign of a trap, but he thought he saw slow movement under the blanket, like a man sleeping peacefully. It might be the wind blowing a blanket tucked around a log, but he didn't think it was. He cocked his rifle. The sound of the shell sliding into the chamber echoed through the night like thunder but did not cause the man under the blanket to stir.

Slocum swung his rifle around when he caught movement out of the corner of his eye. He lowered his Winchester when he saw Borrega step out of the trees at the far side of the clearing. They had their quarry in their sights now.

Slocum gave the high sign. Borrega was quick to act.

"Don't move, you lowdown, no-account varmint," the lawman called. "We got you covered!"

The man under the blanket jerked upright, sending the blanket flapping in the wind like a cavalry pennant. Still more asleep than awake, the man cried out, "Who's there?"

"This is the law, and I'm arrestin' you fer the murder of Micah Underwood."

Slocum stepped out to back up the marshal when he saw the man going for his six-shooter. A quick shot drove the man flat on the ground, his pistol spinning from his nerveless grip.

"Thanks, Slocum," said the marshal coming over and peering down at their captive. "This here's one of Aiken's boys by the name of—"

"Randall," Slocum finished for the lawman. "Randall and I had a run-in back in Denver. He came out second-best there, too." Randall glared up at him, clutching the side where Slocum had grazed him with his bullet.

"Go to hell, Slocum. I shoulda finished the bitch *and* you. I'da done it for nuthin', too."

"Why'd you try to kill Daisy Stevenson?" asked Slocum. He motioned the marshal to silence. He wanted to find out what was going on.

"She confused me. I thought she'd already done her business in the bank and was comin' out. Aiken wanted her dead so she couldn't tell nobody about the bank or the account where he's stashin' the money he's bilkin' from all them fools in Victory."

"So it is a scam?" asked Borrega. "There's no gold in the Mother Lode Mine?"

"Ain't never been, ain't never will be. The gold mine's them fools givin' their hard-earned money to a crook like Aiken. He's takin' 'em all for a fortune to keep that hussy wife of his happy."

"And his mistresses," Slocum added. Randall glared at him, giving him all the answer he needed.

"You plugged the editor on Aiken's orders?" demanded Borrega.

"Why else would I shoot him? I cain't read. Don't matter none what he wrote. Aiken promised me an extra hunnerd dollars. I was supposed to burn down the newspaper office, too, but Slocum was there, then you showed up and everything went to hell real quick."

Randall fell silent as he clutched his injured side. The rising wind sounded like a banshee now, forcing Slocum to grab to keep his hat on his head. As he reached for the brim, Borrega stiffened and half turned in his direction. The look of surprise on the lawman's face puzzled Slocum.

"What's wrong, Marshal?"

"I been shot."

The howling wind died and Slocum heard the telltale sound of a six-shooter cocking again. He stepped away to see behind the marshal. His night-adapted eyes were dazzled by the brilliant flash from the muzzle of a pistol. He fired at the gun but missed. A second bullet ripped out.

"Get down," Slocum called.

"I'm tryin', man, I'm tryin'," grated out the marshal. "I'll secure our prisoner. You get that other backshooter."

Slocum glanced at Randall and knew there wouldn't be any call to hog-tie him. He had been shot smack in the middle of the forehead by the sniper out in the bush.

Falling flat on his belly, Slocum began methodically firing into the undergrowth where the bushwhacker had been. But when his magazine came up empty, he knew he was firing blindly into the night at nothing. The sniper had hightailed it.

"He's dead, isn't he?" Slocum asked the marshal.

"Deader 'n a mackerel," Borrega said weakly. "And I'm not feelin' so good myself."

Slocum went to the lawman's side and ripped away the bloody shirt. The amount of blood staining his shirt and vest astounded Slocum. How could any living man have so much in him? The answer came quick enough.

Borrega was dead.

Standing, Slocum stared at the marshal and the dead outlaw. Success had been snatched away by a sniper's bullet. Randall had confessed everything needed to lock up Basil Aiken in front of a witness. Now both the marshal and the outlaw were dead. Slocum heaved the marshal over his shoulder, ignored the blood soaking into his coat and then draped the corpse over his saddle. He found Randall's horse and duplicated the effort.

He cursed himself for not being more suspicious about why Randall would run like a scalded dog from Victory and then curl up for a nap. The answer now was obvious. He was meeting someone. Slocum didn't have to be much of a fortune-teller to suspect that Zach Hubbell was the gunman who had done so much damage, both to his partner and to Marshal Borrega.

He rode slowly up the canyon and rounded the bend Borrega had mentioned. Stretching in front of him was Green Valley, still cloaked in night. From the evidence given by his watch, it was almost daybreak, but the thick clouds and gathering storm blowing down from higher elevations warned Slocum he ought to find some shelter.

As he entered the valley, he saw the three deputies come riding up, waving their arms like windmill blades in a high wind.

"Slocum, Slocum, he rode past us. We tried to stop 'im, but he shot at us and—" The deputy doing all the talking saw the horses Slocum led—and their burdens.

"It was Zach Hubbell who came riding out like a bat out of hell, wasn't it?" He read the answer in their stunned faces. "He shot the marshal in the back and then killed his partner. Randall confessed everything, but it doesn't mean a thing. My word against . . . the real crooks."

"What are we supposed to do?"

"Which way did Hubbell ride?" Slocum followed their eyes. Hubbell had ridden along the hills defining the valley, probably intending to get himself lost in the rocky terrain.

Knowing the deputies wouldn't be reliable, Slocum passed over the reins of the marshal's horse and said, "Take him back to town. See that he gets a good funeral. As far as Randall goes, I don't care if you leave him out for the dogs to eat."

"He kilt the editor? Randall kilt him?"

"He confessed, for all the good that does," Slocum said.

"Y-you want us to ride with y-you? After Hubbell?" asked another.

"No need. I can travel faster alone." He saw the relief spread over the three men's faces. "Get the marshal back to town now. I'll bring in Hubbell."

"Reckon you can do it," said another. "You was deputized just like we was."

"There's a storm coming. Better get on the trail now," Slocum said. "You have any food? Any supplies?"

The three rooted around in their saddlebags like hesitant hogs and finally, reluctantly, passed over what little they had. Slocum stashed it in his saddlebags and bid them a speedy trip back to Victory. Then he rode in the direction they had indicated that Hubbell had taken. Within a quarter mile the tracks began to fade as Hubbell deliberately rode on rockier stretches, but Slocum saw a notch in the mountains and figured this had to be Hubbell's destination. He picked up the pace, the storm beginning to throw tiny wet snow pellets into his face.

Bandanna pulled up to protect his face, Slocum tugged his hat lower on his forehead and bent down. The brunt of the wind hit the crown of his hat, forcing it hard down onto his head. Following Hubbell became more a matter of faith than skill since snow drifted relentlessly across the terrain now. Slocum reached the pass and took time to eat some of the provender he had borrowed from the other deputies.

Gnawing on a hunk of jerky and drinking from his canteen, Slocum thought about how hard it was going to be running Zach Hubbell to ground. From the way he had lit out after killing the marshal and Randall, Hubbell intended to vanish. Whatever Aiken was paying him wouldn't be enough to keep him in Victory, not with the promise of a gallows a distinct possibility. The best Slocum could tell, Hubbell headed south. Maybe only to New Mexico Territory but more likely to Mexico where it was warm, the señoritas willing, and the tequila abundant.

At least, this is what Slocum would do if their positions had been reversed.

He brushed off the last crumbs of his paltry meal from his lips, licked off his fingers and pulled himself into the saddle. The roan complained but stoutly began walking along the trail over the mountains again. The snow increased to the point where Slocum considered finding a spot to ride out the storm, but he kept moving for another hour before the cold, the snow—the blizzard—forced him to seek shelter in a deep cave large enough for both him and his horse.

Slocum approached the cave cautiously, wiping snow from his eyes. He took a deep whiff, then relaxed. No scent of bear. The last thing he wanted was to share his temporary quarters with a bear preparing to hibernate, though it was still a mite early in the season. Calming his horse, Slocum went to find some dried limbs from nearby dead pine trees. It took the better part of an hour fighting the elements, but he gathered enough firewood to last for a day, built a small firepit and then got the fire blazing merrily.

He sat and warmed his hands. His body felt as if he had been herding cattle all day, aching and stiff and threatening to become worse. Slocum stared out the mouth of the cave at the blowing snow and knew this was going to last awhile. A day or longer. It was unusual, but not unheard of, for such a strong storm this early in the season. The Rocky Mountains were treacherous, but the storm had given plenty of warning.

Slocum pulled his saddle blanket around him and dozed

on and off, the soft whinny of his horse and the whine of wind his constant companions. When he awoke, he had to check his watch to see what time it was.

"Eight o'clock," he muttered. "Morning or evening?" Blanket still tightly wrapped around his shoulders, he ventured to the mouth of the cave and looked out. The heavy snow had petered out to fitful blowing snow, but it was still dark. From the drifts, the embers in his fire and the hunger building in his belly, Slocum guessed it was eight at night. He returned to the fire, built it up, then fixed more food, wishing he had something more for his horse.

He melted what snow he could to water the roan, then drifted back to sleep. This time he awoke to bright sun reflecting off a snow-clad world. Slocum stretched his cramped muscles, draped the blanket back over his horse and then ventured to the mouth of the cave. Traveling through the foot or more of newly fallen snow would be a chore, but Slocum felt up to it if it meant bringing Zach Hubbell back to Victory where he could spill his guts and indict Aiken.

He ate again, this time conserving as much of his sparse larder as he could, saddled and led the horse from the cave through the snow drifts, back to the trail he had followed before. He found some juicy grass poking through the snow and let his horse eat, chafing at the delay. The horse and its continued strength would deliver him his quarry, but he was anxious to get after Hubbell. The horse finally finished.

Slocum swung into the saddle and made his way slowly, occasionally dismounting and leading the horse, until they reached a spot where the hair rose on the back of Slocum's neck. He had stayed alive paying attention to this sixth sense. Danger didn't threaten; this didn't feel to him like someone trained a rifle on him. But somebody was close.

It had to be Zach Hubbell. Slocum tethered the horse, pulled his rifle from its sheath and then took time to reload and tuck the remainder of the cartridges into his coat pocket before going scouting. He struggled through waist-deep drifts until he got to a pile of boulders giving a decent view of the territory.

The first thing he spotted was a fitful curl of black, greasy smoke rising from a spot not thirty yards distant. Making his way through the snow took the better part of a half hour, but Slocum moved quietly until he got into position above the camp where the fire had died out.

The smoke came more from snow blowing across the embers than from green branches being burned. Slocum saw a man sitting, back to a rock, knees drawn up to his chest and head resting on his knees. He sighted in and called, "Hands up, Hubbell. Give up and I won't cut you down."

No movement. Not even a twitch.

Lowering his rifle, Slocum approached cautiously from the side, but he suspected he knew what had happened. He poked Hubbell hard with his rifle barrel. The man fell onto his side, but his arms and legs did not straighten.

Zach Hubbell had frozen to death during the storm.

# 16

The ride back to Victory was harder than Slocum anticipated. In spite of the crystal clear bright blue sky and the
moderating temperatures, the snow melted quickly and
caused fetlock-deep mud for his horse to slog through.
Rather than force the horse to hurry, Slocum let it pick its
way and go slowly. This was especially necessary because
of the added burden draped over the horse's hindquarters.
Hubbell's horse had also frozen to death, forcing Slocum
to decide whether to bury the owlhoot where he had died or
cart him back to town.

Showing Aiken's second henchman as responsible for
the marshal's death was important, but Slocum knew he
had little chance to outargue the mining magnate. Basil
Aiken still commanded a modicum of admiration—and
fed the townspeople's greed—making any accusation
weaker. If only Marshal Borrega had survived, they could
have seen Aiken get his comeuppance.

It took three days of wading through half-frozen mud
before Slocum reached the outskirts of Victory. He wasn't
sure what to expect when he got back since Aiken would
have had days to prepare his speeches and denials. But
when a few people spotted Slocum riding slowly down the

middle of the main street, he received a greeting that was completely unexpected.

"There he is. There's Slocum! He's back!"

The cry spread like wildfire through the town, bringing the citizens out into the muddy streets to cheer and shout, as if he were the president of the United States come to grace Colorado with his presence.

"Yea, Slocum! Hip-hip-hooray!"

Slocum frowned. He hadn't anticipated this at all. Men dragged out crudely lettered banners and tried to hang them on storefronts, mostly failing. The banners fell and were quickly muddied to illegibility, but Slocum saw they had carried sentiments like "hero" and "man of the hour."

He found himself waving, as if he were riding at the head of a parade, but Slocum knew all that lay behind him was the half-frozen dead body of Zach Hubbell.

"You're a peach, Slocum!" shouted a man standing in the doorway of the Sweetwater Saloon. "I'll drink to you anytime!"

From his look, the man would drink to about anything, but Slocum smiled and waved as he rode on, finally stopping in front of the marshal's office. Borrega was dead but someone else must have been appointed marshal by now. After all, Slocum had been four days on the trail.

"Oh, John, you're wonderful!"

Slocum took two steps back and found himself pinned against the jailhouse wall, his arms full of wiggling, warm Daisy Stevenson. In spite of being so public, she planted a big, wet kiss on his lips.

"What's going on?" he asked, finally getting his hands around her waist and lifting her off her feet enough to swing her around. "The town's acting like I've done something."

"You have, you have! The posse returned with the marshal's body and Randall's, too," she added with some distaste. "They told everyone how you shot it out with Randall and tried to save the marshal and couldn't and then went after the man who killed him and now you're back."

"With Zach Hubbell," Slocum managed to get in when Daisy stopped to suck in a breath.

"That's what we figured, in spite of everything Mr. Aiken was saying. How could two of his most trusted men have gone so wrong? Never mind. You brought them to justice."

"Reckon so, since they're both dead. Randall killed Micah Underwood and Hubbell gunned down the marshal."

"You saved the city the cost of tryin' 'n hangin' them weasels," said the barkeep from the Sweetwater Saloon. "My name's Lem and I'm mayor of Victory."

"Congratulations," Slocum said dryly. "You get the body of Hubbell, unless there's a new marshal."

"Strange you should mention that, Slocum. There is a new marshal."

Slocum tensed when he saw the smile on Daisy's face and the stupid grin on Lem's.

"Who might that be?"

"You, Slocum, you. Here's the badge." Lem stepped forward to pin the marshal's badge on Slocum's coat. Slocum was too quick for him, moving aside.

"Not me. I've done my civic duty and there it ends," Slocum said firmly.

"We need you, Slocum," pleaded the mayor. "Victory's a growin' town and we got more cantankerous galoots showin' up every day. We need somebody hard as nails to keep 'em in line. And to run down those intent on serious crimes."

"Not my cup of tea," Slocum said. "I aim to take up prospecting again and make another fortune." He thought this would appeal enough to the owner of the saloon to convince him to stop trying to pin the badge on his chest.

"You can make a fair amount of money. Half the fines for petty crimes and misdemeanors is all yours."

Slocum knew this was the problem with most marshals. They made most of their money from fines and serving process, collecting taxes and foreclosing on property. Running down serious criminals like robbers and killers carried no extra money with it, especially if the crooks got sent to prison somewhere else. Slocum had seen how Borrega used his short-term prisoners to do chores around town. It was usually the marshal's job to remove dead animals and keep the streets in good condition. Having prisoners do this eased the burden on the lawman.

Slocum knew there was only one crook he wanted to bring to justice and that was Basil Aiken. Wearing a badge would hinder him with myriad other duties when bringing down Aiken would require all his attention.

"You sure, Slocum? Folks here are gonna be mighty disappointed. They had their hearts set on you being marshal."

"They'll get over their disappointment," Slocum said. From the corner of his eye he saw how crestfallen Daisy was, too. The blonde would get over it, also—Slocum would see to that. Every minute of the long ride back to Victory not filled with thoughts of how he was going to stop Aiken had been filled with thoughts of Daisy Stevenson.

"Well, I can take this frozen son of a bitch—excuse my language, Miss Stevenson—down to the undertaker. No money to plant him all decent."

"The potter's field is too good for him. I would have left him for the coyotes but wanted everyone to see the man who shot Marshal Borrega in the back."

"We'll make sure folks show up to spit on the grave. Then we can forget him."

"Sounds good."

"You want a drink, Slocum? That's the least I can do since you brung in the man who killed our marshal."

"I'm tuckered out," Slocum said, his eyes locking with Daisy's bright blue ones. He had been in the saddle for four days but that was his lot in life. The snowstorm had been uncomfortable but with the supplies he had cadged from the rest of the posse, he hadn't been in any serious danger. Mostly, he wanted to be alone. With Daisy.

"You go rest up. I think the town fathers want to throw you a bash. Tonight. The Sweetwater, around sundown. Drinks'll be on the house."

"Sunset's coming earlier now," Slocum said.

"Yeah," Lem said, grinning. "Longer nights mean longer time to drink."

The bartender-mayor grunted as he slid Hubbell from Slocum's horse, then kicked and dragged the body to one side of the jailhouse before going off to fetch the undertaker. Lem whistled as he walked away, a spring to his step that told of optimism.

"Oh, John, I wish you'd accepted. Everyone in town thought you would."

"I'm not the kind to cotton much to being a lawman," Slocum said.

She took his arm and rested her cheek against his arm. Even through his coat he could tell her flesh was warm. It was certainly more inviting by the minute. When Daisy looked up and smiled her wicked little smile, Slocum felt himself responding.

"Lem hit the nail on the head when he said I ought to get some rest," Slocum said.

"Did he say that? I seem to remember you being the one who said that," she teased.

"Just goes to show how much I'm in need of finding a good bed and spending some time in it. Sleeping on rocks puts a kink in my back."

"Were you thinking of me?" Daisy asked. They started walking toward her cabin at the edge of town.

"Why're you asking?"

"I wanted to know if the rocks were the only hard thing you were sleeping on."

"Might be something else bothered me. It got lonely out on the trail."

"Then I'm glad you came back to Victory, because you won't be lonely now." Daisy stood on tiptoe and kissed him again. Slocum knew the townspeople, especially the women, would be outraged at such brazen behavior but he didn't much care at the moment. Daisy fit perfectly into the circle of his arm and her body pressed warmly against his, her face upturned for yet another kiss. He gave it to her.

"Let's do it here in the road," she whispered hotly.

"That's better than a parade for my homecoming," Slocum said. He kept his arm around her as she pushed and tried to get away, mock anger flashing across her face. But he read the lust in her cornflower blue eyes. She wanted him as much as he did her.

"Come on. Race you to the cabin."

"Think you can beat me?" he asked.

"Of course I can," she said, smiling at him. "Because you'll want to watch."

"Watch what?" Slocum quickly found out when Daisy stripped off her light jacket and cast it to the muddy ground. He bent and picked it up, giving her a head start of several yards. By the time he caught up, she had already peeled off her blouse.

"Not in public," he called, then bit his tongue. Drawing attention to what they were doing wasn't right. Daisy whirled about, her breasts pressing impudently against her thin undergarment. He saw the tight, taut nubs of her nipples pressing hard against the thin white fabric. She tossed her blouse in his direction.

Slocum made a quick grab and caught it before the garment could fall into the mud. By the time he recovered his balance from the grab, Daisy was just inside the door of the small cabin. She stood with her feet widespread as she fingered open the button holding her skirt. It slithered down around her slender legs and piled around her ankles. She was dressed in nothing but the paper-thin linen undergarment.

Then even this was gone.

She bunched it up and tossed it toward Slocum. He almost dropped it because he couldn't take his eyes off the lovely, naked woman outlined by the rough-hewn wood doorjamb.

Slocum let out a wolf whistle and said, "This is about the prettiest sight I ever did see."

"It gets better," Daisy said, turning. She bent over, her snowy white behind poking out in Slocum's direction. Then the door slammed shut, cutting off his view of such a tempting target. Slocum rushed forward, fumbling to hold on to the woman's clothing she had discarded so wantonly on her way to the cabin.

When he opened the door, he saw an even more delectable sight. Daisy was perched on the table, her feet hiked up to the edge, her knees wide so she was completely exposed.

"See?" she taunted. "It did get better. Now get over here and do something about it! I'm so horny I can hardly stand another second without you!" She opened her knees even more, giving Slocum a look at forbidden territory that caused him to grin wolfishly. He slammed the door behind him and began shedding his unwanted clothes even faster than Daisy had.

"Don't bother getting out of the jeans," she said breathlessly. "I can't wait. Hurry, John, hurry!"

He tossed aside his gun belt and shirt, let his pants fall down to his ankles and hobbled forward, his meaty shaft hard and probing ahead of him as he neared the woman. She grabbed his shoulders and pulled him even closer until the throbbing tip of his manhood brushed across the blond furred mat between her thighs.

Slocum gulped in reaction. The woman's heat, her nearness, her unutterable sexiness and the long, lonely hours he had spent on the trail getting here robbed him of the desire to make this lovemaking last. He wanted her. Bad.

His hands stroked down the outsides of her legs, slid around back and cupped her buttocks. He pulled her forward powerfully. Daisy scooted across the table, her legs widening even more as Slocum fit himself between them. Their crotches ground together for a moment. She threw her head back, her blond hair looking like a golden spray in the sunlight filtering through the cabin window.

For a moment, Slocum felt himself rub along the open curtains hiding the woman's deepest recess. Then he slipped fully forward, her heat and moistness surrounding him completely. Slocum went weak in the knees, then straightened. He lifted powerfully, rocking the blonde back on the table so he could plunge even deeper into her hot core.

"Oh, yes, yes," she moaned. Her eyelids fluttered as she leaned back, supporting herself on her elbows. She reached over and caught her own nips, teasing and toying with them, squeezing powerfully between her thumbs and forefingers. The sight of how she stimulated herself drove Slocum on.

He began a circular motion, stirring his hard shaft around within her tightness. Hands gripped her doughy rump and squeezed down powerfully. Then he tried to move those fleshy lumps in different directions. Daisy caught her breath, flopped flat on her back and stared at the ceiling. Her eyes had glazed over with stark emotion.

"More, more," she grated out. "I need more."

Slocum grunted. She used her powerful inner muscles to clamp down on him, making it feel as if a velvet gloved hand played with his hidden shaft. He pulled back until only the purpled arrowhead at the tip of his manhood remained within, then he shoved forward again, faster than before but still not with the full power of his hips.

The increased movement warmed them both even more. He massaged and kneaded and stroked over her buttocks, then reached up and cupped her breasts. Her hands covered his, holding them in place. They filled his grip, throbbingly alive and exciting him to the point where he could not continue the slow, methodical movement in and out.

He retreated and then replaced himself faster now. The heat from her insides spread throughout his length, stabbing down into his loins and spreading like wildfire throughout his body. Sweat caused by the erotic activity sheened his powerful chest. His breathing became ragged. He stroked and squeezed her breasts and pistoned forward and back and began to move like a locomotive. Every movement now was short of stroke, powerful and increasingly quick.

Slocum rammed in, rotated his hips, then withdrew. Faster he moved. Harder. Deeper. The carnal friction mounted. He was aware of how the woman's long legs wrapped around his waist, her ankles locked behind his back. He moved faster and faster until his hips flew like a shuttlecock. Then the woman shrieked in a sudden release of desire.

He thought she would squeeze him flat as her strong inner muscles clamped down hard. Then he didn't notice. The white-hot tide from deep within rose, hesitated and then exploded. Slocum slammed hard into the willing, wanton woman and all too soon sank down. Daisy's legs were already dangling limply over the edge of the table.

Slocum laid his head on her breasts, twisted and lightly kissed each in turn before standing up again.

"Oh, it went away," Daisy said with mock sorrow. "Can I help get it back? My little friend?"

"Not so little," Slocum said.

"It is now, but let me see if I can talk it into coming back even bigger and harder." Daisy slithered off the table and sank to her knees in front of Slocum, taking him first in her hands and then her mouth. The way her lips worked on his exhausted organ was beginning to cause new stirrings of desire when Slocum heard a horse whinny outside.

Reluctantly, he reached down and pushed Daisy away. "Someone's coming."

"I know," Daisy said dreamily. "I know two who—"

"Outside. A horse. Get decent!" Slocum was already pulling up his jeans. He was glad he hadn't kicked off his boots now.

It took Daisy a few seconds to hear what he already had. She gasped, grabbed for her own clothes and got both skirt and blouse on, though she misbuttoned the blouse by the time a sharp rap came on the door.

"Sis, you here? I got news!"

"Your brother," Slocum said, still working to get his gun belt strapped on. He considered firing a few times through the door to run off Daisy's obtrusive brother. If he winged the young man, so much better. Slocum was getting tired of being interrupted.

"Andy, wait a moment," Daisy said, hastily shoving her undergarments into a chest and then hastily sitting on it. She tried to smooth her hair into place and failed. "Come on in."

Slocum swung the chair at the table around, straddled it and leaned forward, his forearms resting on the straight back.

Andrew Stevenson came in, a puppy-dog eager look on his face.

"You won't guess what's happened, Sis."

"Hello, Andy," Slocum said. He wondered if the man was dense or if he just couldn't believe his sister would ever enjoy the company of a man that was not her brother.

"Oh, there you are, Mr. Slocum. This is so good. And it involves you, too."

"What is it, Andy?" asked Daisy.

"Well, when Mr. Slocum turned down Lem's offer to be marshal, Mr. Aiken got to thinking who'd be a good choice to replace Borrega."

Slocum sat a little straighter in the chair, his hands gripping the back. He felt as if he stood on railroad tracks and waited for a runaway steam engine.

"What'd he have to say? Mr. Aiken?" asked Daisy.

"He said he knew just the man for the job."

Slocum held his breath as Andy Stevenson opened his coat and showed them the marshal's badge pinned to his shirt.

"I'm the new marshal in Victory. Me!" he exclaimed.

# 17

The howling wind promised another storm laced with rain and snow. Slocum shivered and drew a blanket around his shoulders. The small stove in the corner of the cabin tried its best to keep the occupants warm but failed, no matter how much he stoked it. Slocum looked over at Daisy. The woman went about housekeeping chores, but she looked as if she had gained fifty pounds. She wore every stitch of clothing she had, and it was still only barely enough to keep her warm.

"You and your brother ought to get on back to Denver before winter sets in," Slocum said. "This place is going to be under ten feet of snow in another month."

"Denver isn't as cold, or so it seemed," Daisy allowed. "But then we had rooms with a dozen other people. We'd all chip in for wood and coal to burn in the common room."

"And if enough of you crowded close, that added to the heat."

Daisy smiled wanly.

"You do your part keeping me warm. At night. Sometimes during the day, when you're not out doing whatever you do."

Slocum heard the criticism in her tone. He hadn't bothered telling her most of the time he spent away from the cabin was devoted to following Aiken and Touhy, trying to find what they were up to. Over the long, cold nights since Marshal Borrega had been killed, Slocum had slowly pieced together what was going on, and he didn't much like it. Basil Aiken was cutting off loose ends. Randall had been one, so Aiken had used him to kill another loose end: Micah Underwood. The newspaper editor would have seen to it that his articles followed Aiken throughout Colorado. So he had to die.

Randall had gunned down the newspaperman, then Zach Hubbell had eliminated him. Slocum wondered how Aiken had intended for Hubbell to die. By Touhy's hand? That was possible, but the sudden blizzard had saved Touhy the trouble of murdering his partner. Slocum wondered if Touhy realized how close to death he walked every day. Aiken wasn't the sort to let anyone who knew the inner workings of his scheme remain alive and testify against him.

Slocum snorted and shook his head. Aiken had free rein as long as Andrew Stevenson was marshal. The young man still thought the sun rose and set on the mining magnate. When he wasn't prancing around pretending to be a lawman, Stevenson still sold stock certificates in the worthless mines Aiken touted. Nothing more had come of the claim that the Mother Lode Mine was on Ute land. Slocum was happy for that, because dealing with Bear Tail had become increasingly difficult. The Indian wanted more ponies to continue his claims, knowing Slocum needed his testimony more than anything else.

That Aiken had not resurveyed the land and discovered it did not belong to the Utes told Slocum more than anything else what a swindler the man was. Any man having such a rich gold mine ripped from his grasp would have moved heaven and earth to hold on to it. He might even have dickered directly with Bear Tail, offering a remuda for every brave in his band. A hundred horses ought to have been a small price to pay for such a supposedly rich claim.

"A thousand horses," Slocum snorted. Plumes of condensation gusted from his nose and mouth as he spoke.

"What's that, John?"

"Nothing, just thinking out loud."

"You still selling horses and other animals left at Smitty's livery stables?" she asked.

"Not so many left behind without getting paid for now. And not many new prospectors to sell to," Slocum said.

"It's as if Victory is dying up and blowing away."

"Or being buried," Slocum said. And he didn't mean under snow.

"I need your help," Daisy said. She finished wiping off the table, rubbed her hands on her apron and turned to him. The strained look on her face was accentuated by the paleness caused by the cold. This, as much as anything, convinced Slocum she couldn't stay in Victory much longer—or not in this cabin. When it got really cold, no amount of clothing or burning in the pitiful, small stove would keep her alive.

"If it's help getting back to Denver, I'll be more than happy to oblige."

"Not that. We can't leave. We can't, John. You know that. We're getting rich."

"Rich?" He stood and went to her, draping the blanket over her quaking shoulders. "Are you living rich? Sell some of the stock, use the money to get a better, bigger stove. Stuff paper in the chinks in the walls. Hell, stuff those worthless stock certificates there. That's all they're good for." He wondered how Rip and Gladstone were doing. If their luck had held, their cabin with the old stock certificates from Aiken's prior scam would have been long deserted, the pair of miners living high, wide and happy in Denver.

"That's not true," she said, but for the first time he could remember, Daisy didn't sound too convinced.

She turned from him, obviously having a difficult time asking for the favor. Slocum wasn't inclined to help her out since she so steadfastly refused to give up the hope of getting rich from Aiken's bogus mines.

"It's Andy. I'm real worried about him, John," she blurted out. "Since he pinned that badge on, he's different."

"That much responsibility can make a boy grow up to be a man," Slocum pointed out.

"It's not that. Something's eating at him, and he won't tell me what it is. Every time I ask, he always changes the subject. But it's powerful bad. I can tell it is from the way he's acting."

"What do you want me to do? Follow him around?"

Slocum grunted when she answered. It was as bad as he thought.

"Yes."

"I'll do what I can, but no promises. It might be that the job's bigger than he can handle."

"Find out. If that's true, I'll convince him to resign. Even—" Daisy bit off the rest of her sentence. She turned and grabbed Slocum in a hug, burying her face into the front of his coat. "Even if it means giving up and going back to Denver. I can't see him like this. I promised Ma and Pa to always look after him. And they upped and died and he's all I've got, and I'm all he's got and—"

"I'll see that he's not in any trouble," Slocum said.

Most of the day Andrew Stevenson tended to his marshal's chores around Victory, but when it came to peddling Aiken's stock certificates Stevenson was a tad less eager. Slocum saw several instances of newcomers to Victory, all het up to find gold and become millionaires, who might have been sold a few shares each. Stevenson talked with them and only halfheartedly hawked the stock certificates. Slocum was too far away to hear what was said, the transaction being conducted in front of the general store, but the set to Stevenson's body told the tale. He lacked the enthusiasm he once had.

Slocum had little time to reflect on this. Stevenson swung into the saddle and rode out of town at a brisk clip, forcing Slocum to get his own horse and trail along about a mile back. The roads were half frozen, and the wind picked up as it blew down from higher elevations. The knife-edge in the wind, though, did not warn of a new storm. It was still late fall, but the altitude had worked against much new exploration for gold. Even the land office clerk complained of how slack his business had become due to the weather.

The only one Slocum didn't see complaining was Basil Aiken. The man bustled about, conferred often with Touhy, and spent a good part of his time going from business to business collecting his share of the daily revenues. This told Slocum Aiken was getting ready to simply vanish, having milked as much as he could from the gullible, greedy people of Victory.

He had ridden along without paying much attention to the man he followed. When Stevenson cut off the road suddenly, Slocum had to backtrack and find the small path winding away into the hills. He wasn't sure what lay in this direction, but from the man-sized gopher holes burrowing into the mountains, it was probably another of the "sure-enough-can't-fail" gold fields Aiken had been selling shares in.

The trail looked to be chopped up by the passage of more than Stevenson's horse. Slocum studied the spoor and decided someone had brought a heavily laden mule along here within the past day or two. He heaved a sigh. More prospectors out looking for their elusive will-o'-the-wisp.

"Howdy, mister. You with the marshal?" The voice came from off the trail and startled Slocum. He had been too lost in thought to pay attention to his surroundings. If the prospector hadn't been a friendly sort, Slocum knew he might have been bushwhacked and left for dead.

"I was looking to find him," Slocum said. "Got a message from his sister."

"Oh, Miss Daisy?" The prospector ambled up out of a ravine where he had been out of sight. "The marshal goes on about her a lot. Must be a real looker. All the fellas in town sniffin' 'round after her."

"Not so many," Slocum said. "Not when her brother's the marshal."

The prospector laughed heartily.

"Can't imagine Marshal Stevenson puttin' any kinda fear into a man. You see the way he wears that hogleg of his? He's danged lucky he hasn't shot off his own foot yet." The prospector sobered and wiped his lips. "You and him friends?"

"Just bringing him a message," Slocum assured the man.

"I seen him pass by not more 'n a half hour ago. Goin' on up to the Jackson twins' claim. Again."

"Again? He's up there often?"

"Him and them two talk 'til they're blue in the face."

"What about?" Slocum hooked his leg around his saddle pommel and leaned over a bit, wondering if he ought to dismount. When he saw the prospector had his own mule packed, a decent diamond hitch thrown on the contents, he decided to stay where he was.

"Same as the rest of us, I reckon." The prospector looked over his shoulder and figured Slocum had a good look at his pack mule. "Ain't no gold up here. It took me close to a week to figger that out, but them Jackson twins, they're kinda dense." The prospector tapped the side of his head. "Like they was both kicked in the heads by ole Belle here." He tugged on the bridle and got the mule to take a step or two so he could pat the animal on the neck.

"So you're giving up on looking for gold?"

"Ain't even coal here. I made a fair amount of money off a coal mine up in Middle Park. Sold it to General Palmer so he could run his toy railroad all around the state."

"You sound like a railroad man yourself," Slocum said.

"Was. Worked on the Central Pacific 'til they drove the gold spike up in Utah. Then they didn't need no gang bosses, so I tried my hand at prospectin'." The man looked more closely at Slocum. "You don't have the look of a prospector 'bout you. You Stevenson's deputy?"

Slocum had to laugh.

"No. Wearing a badge isn't for me. I was looking to give the marshal a message."

"You said that. You ain't lookin' to deliver a . . . lead message, now are you? I like him, even if he is as dense as the Jackson twins."

"Nothing like that."

The prospector considered this, Slocum's demeanor and who knows what else before coming to the decision it was all right to talk a bit more.

"The marshal's not goin' to the Jackson twins' claim. He done talked to them last week. He's prob'ly headin' for Colorado Jim's mine. He don't say much 'cuz all he does is work. He bored his shaft a good fifty yards into the side of a mountain."

"And he hasn't found any gold, either," Slocum finished.

"Then you and the marshal have been talkin'," the prospector said, relieved. "That's all he talks on now, how nobody's found a speck of precious metal in these hills. Don't know what it means to him, but what it means to me is I got to get somewhere warmer 'fore winter sinks its teeth into these mountains."

"Getting cold early," Slocum allowed.

"Hope you find the marshal 'fore another storm blows in. Colorado Jim's. Take the left fork, not the right 'less you want to sit all day listenin' to the Jackson boys tell you their life story. Believe me, it ain't worth it."

"Have a safe trip wherever you're going," Slocum said.

"Thanks." The prospector tugged on Belle's bridle and got the mule going. The pack animal walked along briskly, obviously as eager as her owner wanting to get out of the cold and find warmer climes.

Slocum unhooked his leg and headed uphill, into the mountains where the majority of the new claims had been sold. He got his bearings and decided this was the southern end of the claim he had sold to Aiken—had used extortion to sell. Instinctively, his hand went to his shirt pocket. He still had most of the money left, in spite of the boomtown prices in Victory. It would give him a stake for the next year, if he didn't spend wildly and chose his poker games carefully.

He found the fork in the road and took the one toward Colorado Jim's mine, although most of the tracks veered in the other direction to the one owned by the Jackson brothers. Slocum reached a point in a narrow gully where he heard voices—many voices—all yammering at once. He thought it might be the peculiar echoing effect caused by the high rock walls and narrow ravine, then he realized the men were arguing.

Putting his heels to his roan's flanks, he hastened along the trail and reached a point where he could look down on the mine. A half-dozen horses, mostly looking broke down, and mules were tethered downhill from Colorado Jim's mine. The men sat around a bonfire, warming their hands and each other's ears with their hot invective.

Slocum listened and made out the gist of the little pow-wow going on. He had misjudged Andy Stevenson. After Aiken had pinned on the marshal's badge, Slocum thought Stevenson would be the man's lapdog. Everything he heard proved different. Stevenson had been riding through the claims, talking to the owners and finding not a one of them had discovered a trace of gold. He had called a meeting of nearby mine owners and was getting an earful of their complaints.

Stevenson carefully noted everything in a small ledger, nodding on occasion and shouting for the miners to quiet down so he could listen to them one at a time.

Slocum knew Andrew Stevenson had figured out how crooked Aiken was. Would he be able to convince his sister? Tugging on his reins, Slocum turned his horse's face and headed back to Victory. There was likely to be all sorts of trouble if—when—the new marshal decided to arrest Basil Aiken.

# 18

Slocum drew rein and looked at Daisy's cabin. Her brother's horse was tethered out back, trying vainly to drink through the ice on the watering trough. Slocum dismounted, broke the ice for Stevenson's horse and his own, then wondered if he ought to interrupt. Since he knew what Stevenson had been up to as he made his rounds as marshal, he decided against it. Let the fledgling marshal try to convince Daisy that Aiken was a crook. Stevenson certainly had the information from most of the miners in surrounding areas, including the claim Slocum had sold to Aiken.

It was all a fraud, and since Slocum couldn't convince the woman, her brother might.

Slocum sauntered down the street toward the Sweetwater Saloon. Smitty was inside, getting drunker by the minute.

"Slocum, ole buddy, come on in. Set yerse'f down and have a drink. On me!"

"What's the occasion?" asked Slocum. "You don't buy drinks for anyone."

"Sold my stables."

"To Aiken?"

"Him? Ha! That son of a bitch wouldn't pay for tendin'

his horses. Came close to turnin' them nags o'er to you more 'n once."

"Do tell." Slocum settled into a chair opposite the former livery stable owner and signalled Lem for a beer. "How long has he been shortchanging you?"

"Ever since he come to town. Thass why I knowed he was a deadbeat. Wouldn't pay." Smitty downed his shot of rye whiskey and had Lem bring him another. "I'm well done with Victory. Time to move on. Can't go west. Not with storms comin' fast and furious, so I'm headin' south. Maybe to Santa Fe or even Mesilla. Find me one of them willin' young señoritas. Did I say I wanted a young one?"

"Good idea. It's getting colder here by the day, and it's not even winter yet."

"These ole bones're too old to stay much longer. Come 'long with me, Slocum. We make a good team."

Slocum was amused by the stable owner's drunken request.

"I'd like to, Smitty, but I've got things to do and none of them are to the south."

"Hell, we kin go east. There's gotta be some young, willin' young ladies out that way." Smitty belched and then shook his head. "Wait a minute. You got yerse'f one aw'ready. Well, good fer you, Slocum. I'll drink to you and the purty little filly!"

Slocum banged his mug to Smitty's shot glass and downed the beer. Lem had no trouble keeping the beer cold now. If anything, Slocum might have preferred a hot cup of coffee, if there'd been one available. He was starting on his second beer when he saw Daisy outside, gesturing to him.

"If I don't see you before you leave, Smitty, you find yourself a pretty little Mexican spitfire."

"Young," Smitty said. "She's gotta be young."

Slocum laughed, then pushed through the doors to the boardwalk.

"John, I didn't know where to find you."

"What's wrong?"

"I . . . Andy wants to talk to you. There's something brewing, and he doesn't know what to do."

"Tell me about it," Slocum said, knowing Daisy's brother would never get to the point. As they walked in the direction of her cabin, Daisy fidgeted and fussed. A slight stutter returned to her talk.

"I t-think Aiken might try to kill me again. He's asked if I can take m-more m-money to Denver and deposit it for him. Says I'm the only one in Victory he trusts."

"Did he tell you it was money?"

"No, but I thought it must be like last time. And last time Randall tried to kill me. It was Randall, wasn't it?"

Slocum's mind raced. Aiken was finishing off his dirty business in Victory and had to count Daisy as a loose end. A very loose end. But would he try the identical stunt, the one that had failed before? The only dependable man he had left working with him was Touhy.

"He just told you to courier a package to Denver? He didn't actually say there was money in the case, did he?"

"N-no, but I thought—"

"What's your brother planning to do?"

"He—he wants me to do it."

"Why's that?" Slocum got a cold knot in his belly. This sounded as if Stevenson was planning on doing something that would get him in plenty of hot water. Because a man wore a badge didn't make him a lawman. Most of the marshals and sheriffs that Slocum knew had spent more time on the other side of the law. They were perfectly suited to keep the law because they knew all the ways to break it—usually from firsthand experience. Andrew Stevenson was a babe in the woods in comparison, which was why Aiken had insisted on him taking the vacant job.

They went into the cabin, seemingly even smaller now that all three of them in heavy coats crowded inside. Stevenson sat on the bed looking morose. He glanced up at

Slocum and his expression didn't change, but Slocum thought he saw a flicker of hope in the man's eyes.

"Mr. Slocum, I'm glad Sis found you."

"She told me what you're planning. It's mighty dangerous for her."

"I don't see any other way to flush out Aiken. You've been hintin' all along how crooked he is. I was serving process up in the hills and got to talkin' with the miners. Not a one's found a speck of gold. Not in streams, not in hard rock, not even in your claim."

"I never found any, but I duped Aiken into buying it."

"The Mother Lode Mine's not on Ute land. I did some checking," Stevenson said.

"That's more than Aiken did. That should have alerted everyone that they were being taken for fools," Slocum said. "Instead, they kept buying stock certificates, only this time in *my* claim, and I knew there wasn't any gold on it."

"You're bein' too kind, Mr. Slocum," Stevenson said glumly. "I was the one talkin' them folks into buyin', into spendin' their money on pieces of paper that weren't worth a thing."

"What's your plan?" Slocum asked.

"You go with Sis to Denver, like you did before. Watch her carefully, don't let anythin' happen to her. At the bank, get witnesses to what's being deposited. That money's all gotten by illegitimate means." Stevenson pronounced the words carefully, as if reciting from a law book. "We need more than a few miners with nothin' but worthless rock in their mines to arrest Aiken. He's a slippery devil."

"He's done this before," Slocum said. "He struck it rich a couple times, maybe by skill, probably through good luck, then made even more money selling a dream." He told them of the miners he had talked with before.

"We can get a whole slew of them together at the trial," Stevenson said.

"Might end up getting Aiken lynched."

"Is that so bad?" flared Daisy. "After all he's done!"

"I don't always see eye-to-eye with the law, but I never agreed with a lynch mob. A couple dozen men thinking with half a brain is too dangerous."

"We need evidence. I don't know any other way to get it," Stevenson said.

"I doubt Aiken will send Daisy to Denver with more money. There won't be anything but rocks or old newspaper in the case."

"What else can we do?" Daisy looked adamant. She was going to Denver to collect evidence for her brother, no matter what.

"Not much," Slocum said, bowing to the inevitable. Unless he hog-tied her and watched over her twenty-four hours a day, he wasn't going to change her mind. She was as stubborn as a mule—but a lot better looking.

"We should look," Daisy said. "I've got to know. Is he sending me to Denver with money or just to be killed? He's got the money, so maybe I do have it."

Slocum looked at her out of the corner of his eye. She argued with herself and hardly needed a response, but he felt as if he should say something.

"There's no money in the case," Slocum said firmly. "He just wants to know where you'll be. I suspect Touhy will be waiting outside the bank in Denver, ready to shoot you."

As he spoke, something didn't sound right to him. Aiken was not a stupid man. Randall had failed with the same plan. Why should it succeed a second time when it had failed so badly the first? True, Randall had simply gotten confused and tried to kill Daisy too soon. Aiken would have wanted her to deliver the money, then be killed on the way out of the bank. That put the money in the bank and eliminated the courier who could testify to it later.

Even better, the crime would be committed in Denver,

far from Victory. The people of Victory would believe anything they heard of the big city and its rampant crime.

"Let me look."

"Go on," Slocum said, still trying to figure out what was wrong. He watched as Daisy pulled the heavy suitcase to her lap and then fumbled with the catches. He had never replaced the knife he had given Bear Tail or he would have used it to slice through the thick leather straps and pry open the locks. But he misjudged Daisy's determination. She used a nail file and accomplished the same feat that he could have with a sturdy, thick-bladed knife.

"There," she said with satisfaction at a job well done. Opening the lid, she let out a low whistle. Neatly bundled inside were stacks of greenbacks. "You were wrong," she said in a low voice. Daisy started to close the case but Slocum stopped her. He took a bundle from the middle of the case and showed her that Aiken had placed real scrip on the top of cut newspaper.

"There's hardly a hundred dollars in there. Just the bills you see."

"Why, the sneak! He knew I'd look and when I saw it, I'd close the case and—" Daisy turned pale when the real significance hit her. No money meant Aiken had sent her on a wild-goose chase—and intended for her to be killed.

The train rattled along its narrow-gauge track, then began a steep climb into the mountains not twenty miles from Victory.

"He wants us both dead," Slocum said suddenly. "He's getting rid of everyone who might come after him."

"How, John? There's no way he could ever hope to harm you."

The train shuddered and steamed up an even steeper grade into the mountains. Slocum pushed past Daisy and stood in the aisle. The passengers mostly stared in boredom out the window or slept—hardly a dozen others in the car. The car ahead held more. And all there was behind was the caboose.

"I'll be back in a few minutes," Slocum said. He made his way up the steeply sloping floor and reached the door leading to the platform between cars. The train was almost at the summit and Touhy crouched down, doing something to the heavy coupler connecting the cars.

As Slocum opened the door, a blast of cold air hit him in the face. Touhy looked up, panic replacing concentration. He bent low and fumbled more, jerked back and came up with a greasy connector pin.

"Stop!" Slocum called. He went for his six-shooter, drew and fired as the coupling opened. The passenger car he was in and the caboose slowed and then began gathering speed as they rolled back downhill. The remainder of the train, suddenly freed of the weight, surged forward.

Slocum took better aim this time but there was no call to fire a second time. His first slug had killed Touhy. The man sprawled on the narrow tracks, face in the cinders. He wasn't moving.

But the sensation of speed built, and Slocum realized the danger he and everyone in the rear two cars faced.

"John," cried Daisy. "What happened? Why're we going backward?"

"Brace yourself," Slocum said, running to the rear of the car. Their downhill speed grew. He flung open the door to the rear platform, swung around a low railing and got into the caboose where the conductor and another crewman struggled to get to their feet. Both were already so drunk the slant of the car as it raced back down the tracks made them doubly unsteady on their feet.

"How do you stop it? Where's the brake?" shouted Slocum. The conductor pointed up.

"Outside," was all he got out before Slocum vaulted over him and ran to the rear of the red caboose. He kicked open the door and looked out. The brake could only be applied from the roof.

Wasting no time, Slocum swung around, grabbed the iron rungs of the ladder leading up and got to the roof. Wind whistled fast past him as he looked downhill. The cars were running fast enough now that they might derail if they hit a curve. The railroad bed was narrow, and the chasm to one side was too deep for Slocum to see the bottom. If the cars went over, it would be spring before anyone found their bodies.

Putting his back into it, he began twisting the wheel that applied the brakes to the caboose. The wheel kicked in his hands when he reached the place where metal grated on metal, but he had to keep the pressure on or the cars would never slow, much less stop. Bracing his feet, Slocum used every ounce of strength in his body to turn the braking wheel. The smell of burned metal rose, and the caboose chattered and jumped on the tracks, a fight between gravity and friction offered by the brake.

"Lemme help," called the crewman from the caboose. He almost fell off as he awkwardly climbed the ladder, but he locked one leg around at the top rung and twisted along with Slocum. The cars careened around a turn, smashing into the rocky wall, but they stayed on the tracks. A second collision with a rocky wall shattered windows in both the caboose and passenger car.

Slocum heard the screams of panic from the passengers, then thumps as they were tossed around within the car. He thought of Daisy, helpless, frightened, and his resolve stiffened. He turned even harder, tendons standing out in bold relief on his forearms. Beneath his heavy coat, his shirt split across his shoulders as he applied even more pressure. For long seconds he thought nothing was happening, then the cars lurched and began to slow visibly. The rock wall to the side of the train no longer raced past. They were still speeding along at a reckless pace, but continued application of the brake brought them to a more measured rate.

"Damn me if this ain't workin'," the crewman said, the strain showing on his weathered face. "We're slowin' down. We're actually slowin' this runaway hunk of wood and steel!"

Slocum started to answer, then held his peace. One of the passengers, still fearing the worst, jumped. Unfortunately, he jumped on the wrong side of the train and tumbled head over heels for a few feet before plunging over the sheer precipice on the right side of the cars.

His screams as he tumbled through empty space were drowned out by the sick screech of tearing metal. The brake wheel bucked in Slocum's hands, then allowed him to apply even more pressure.

Bit by bit the cars slowed to a less dangerous speed of descent. When they came to a halt, rocking from side to side, the smell of hot metal was enough to make Slocum sick to his stomach.

The crewman grinned, thrust his calloused hand out, and said, "Put 'er there, partner. Anytime you want a job on the 'road, I'll see you get it. You saved all our bacon."

From the passenger car came cries of joy, sobbing and the inevitable questions of what had happened. There'd be time for all that later.

Slocum shook the man's hand, then sagged down to the roof of the caboose. Sweat poured down his face and got into his eyes. He tried to lift his hand to wipe it off but all his strength was gone. He was left as limp as a dishrag.

# 19

Slocum dropped to the tracks and stared at the ruined wheels on the caboose. They smoked and even from ten feet away he felt the heat radiating powerfully. To touch any of the wheels or the track would cause a nasty burn. He made his way around the banged up cars, edging along the rock wall until he reached the passenger car. The windows had been smashed and parts of the frame were bent or entirely missing.

"Daisy!" he called. "Are you all right?"

"Here I am," came her weak voice. "What happened?"

"The cars came uncoupled," he said, not wanting to get into details. The sight of Touhy lying facedown with a bullet in him was still fresh—but not as vivid as the sight of the car and caboose careening downhill, wobbling from side to side along the narrow tracks, crashing into the rocky wall of the mountain pass. Touhy had obviously intended to kill not only Slocum and Daisy but everyone else. It would have been ruled an accident. Who would release a car in such a fashion?

"Oh, my, glass," the blonde said, sticking her head out a window rimmed with jagged debris. She carefully brushed away the shards remaining in the window, then crawled through. Slocum caught her as she jumped to the ground. She looked up at him, her expression unfathomable. He kissed her, but there was no passion. She clung to him for a moment, then pushed back and stared at him. "It wasn't an accident, was it?"

He shook his head. She rested her cheek against him for a moment longer and pushed away again.

"You're wet."

Slocum laughed without humor. He had sweated buckets working the brake. The device had never been designed to stop a runaway caboose but only to hold it stationary on a siding. The effort applying the brake had sucked everything out of him, sweat and strength.

"We've got to get back to Victory," Slocum said. "Touhy was supposed to kill us. When Aiken finds he failed, he'll hightail it and we'll never catch him."

Daisy got a faraway look in her eyes as she nodded.

"There's money. Plenty of money somewhere," she said. "If he wasn't actually sending it with me to deposit in the Denver bank, he's still got it. In Victory. Somewhere."

"Don't worry about that." Slocum looked back uphill, but the train had steamed on without its last two cars. He doubted the engineer would stop and send any of the crew back to see what had caused the passenger car and caboose to go rattling backward down the steep grade. He would continue on, maybe to Pueblo or Colorado City before alerting his superiors. It might be a day before another train came back along this section of track.

"You're right about returning," Daisy said. "We have to warn Andy."

"He be all right for a spell," Slocum said, thinking hard. "Nothing'll happen until Aiken finds we're not dead."

"How many miles is it?" Daisy asked.

"We were on the train for a half hour. That makes it a good ten, fifteen miles back to town. It might be as many as twenty, but it's all downhill."

"Let's start walking. We can get back by sundown."

Slocum shook his head.

"There's no way we can make that kind of time on foot. It'll be midnight, not dusk. Maybe even sometime tomorrow morning, if we don't make good time. And it's getting colder, if you hadn't noticed." Wind blew along the tracks, wending down from higher, more frigid altitudes. "We should wait for the return train."

"No." Daisy jerked free and began walking. She ignored the conductor and the crewman in the caboose. Slocum waved to them and hurried after her. It was a long way back, and it was going to get mighty cold if snow joined the wind.

Their luck turned for the better when Slocum found a handcar a mile down the road. It took them the better part of a half hour to wrestle it onto the tracks, but pumping rhythmically sent the small car sailing back toward Victory. Daisy proved to be right. They reached the railroad depot just after sundown.

"Didn't you folks leave on the morning train?" asked the ticket agent and station master, standing on the edge of the platform, watching as Slocum and Daisy jumped down from the handcar, exhausted from their daylong hardship on the rails.

"We did. There was trouble with the coupling on a passenger car. You might send a telegram to the railroad home office and let them know," Slocum said.

"Well," the stationmaster said, shuffling his feet. Slocum walked over to him and peered down, fixing him with his cold green eyes.

"What's happened here in town while we were gone?" Slocum demanded. Daisy rushed to his side and grabbed his arm.

"Don't tell me. I-it's my brother, isn't it?"

Slocum had the same gut feeling. The agent nodded, swallowed hard, then got his words all in a line. He spat them out like a Gatling gun firing a full magazine.

"It happened this afternoon, don't know the details. The marshal's dead, shot in the back, mighta been a drunk over at the Sweetwater Saloon." The stationmaster stepped away and looked as if he expected Slocum to take a swing at him.

Slocum and Daisy turned as one and ran all the way to the saloon. There was a moderate-sized crowd standing on the boardwalk in front, spillover from the larger crowd within.

"Lem!" Slocum called. "Lem!"

"Slocum," came the mayor-bar owner's reply. "Get on in here. You got Miss Stevenson with you?"

Slocum forced his way inside. The weather outside was turning cold and blustery, promising more snow, but in the saloon it was more like a blast furnace. Too many unwashed bodies crowded in, but Slocum got through as he led Daisy to the bar.

"What happened?" Slocum demanded.

Lem inclined his head toward the back of the saloon. The crowd parted as if by magic and Slocum got a good view of Andrew Stevenson laid out on the pool table, Basil Aiken standing beside him. Shock flashed on Aiken's face, quickly replaced with a poker face that might have been chiseled from granite. The mining magnate and Slocum stared at each other, but Aiken broke the silent contest of wills.

"Miss Stevenson!" he called, waving expansively. "Let me offer my condolences on this sad, sorry day." Daisy advanced on leaden feet, her eyes fixed on her brother's corpse. "I feel responsible for poor Andrew's death, having been the one who urged him to become marshal. But he died nobly in the discharge of his duties, protecting all of us in Victory."

"Shot in the back?" was all Daisy got out. Her words were hardly louder than a whisper.

"My dear, Andrew was a fine man, a true gentleman and

has been robbed of a bright and prosperous future. As a token of his achievement, I gave Andrew these. Please accept them in memory of his goodness." Aiken held out his hand. Daisy mechanically extended hers. Aiken dropped the two gold bullets he had presented to her brother.

Daisy stared at them before looking up at Aiken. Tears filled her eyes, then she turned and ran from the saloon. Slocum half turned, then reconsidered and let her go. His business was with Basil Aiken. But the crowd surged and pushed Slocum away, pinning him against the bar for long minutes. By the time he forced his way through to the pool table, Aiken had disappeared. He started toward the back door but Lem's hand grabbed him and swung him around.

"Slocum, in my role as mayor of this here town, I got to ask."

"I don't want to be marshal," Slocum said, looking over the heads of the men as he tried to spot Aiken.

"That ain't the problem. Didn't think you'd reconsider. We got a problem with buryin' the boy. He worked for the town but we ain't got spit left in the treasury, thanks to Borrega and him dippin' into the till to buy Aiken's stock certificates. Hate to wrap young Stevenson in a blanket. Deserves a coffin, but he ain't gettin' any more unless . . ." Lem's voice trailed off. Slocum fumbled in his pocket, peeled off twenty in greenbacks and handed it to the mayor. Lem took it and said, "Much obliged. We'll see he gets a right nice headstone, too."

Slocum finally got free and burst out the back door into the alley behind the saloon. He looked around but didn't see the man. Slocum decided there was no hurry tracking down Aiken and turned toward Daisy's cabin. But as he walked toward the small shack, he saw that the freshly falling snow was unblemished with footprints. Slocum stopped, turned and looked back into town. The snow fell more heavily now, obscuring the buildings behind a swirling white, wet curtain.

He trudged back down the main street, heading for the Mother Lode Mining Company office, hunting for Basil Aiken. Slocum drew his six-shooter when he saw the front door standing ajar. Snow blew into the fancy office, drifting enough to outline footprints.

Two sets went in, only one came out.

From the size of those leaving, Slocum guessed they belonged to a woman. A woman about Daisy's size. He pushed open the door the rest of the way using the barrel of his six-gun, then slipped inside. A long step carried him over the snow piling on the floor. Slocum had no intention of leaving a new set of footprints for whoever became the new marshal.

"Aiken?" Slocum's voice echoed in the darkened room. He studied the shadows in the corners, expecting the mining magnate to appear suddenly, six-shooter blazing. He cocked his head to one side and listened. All he heard was the groaning of the wood walls as nails cooled and pulled out and the rising whine of the storm outside.

"Aiken?"

Slocum moved along the wall a few feet, then stopped. He caught sight of a foot sticking out from under the large, ornate desk. With a quick move, he kicked the desk chair out of the way to expose Basil Aiken on the floor. Slocum didn't have to check to be sure the man was dead, but he did anyway. Rolling him over, Slocum saw two small holes over Aiken's heart. Whoever had shot him had been close. The cloth of Aiken's vest had burned from the discharge.

Peering closer, Slocum saw something peculiar about the residue on the vest. Along with the partially burned gunpowder shone a smear of gold.

Slocum pulled the body out from under the desk and heard a loud clank as metal hit the floor. He bent over Aiken and picked up a familiar derringer. It was the one he had given Daisy for protection. Slocum ran his finger around the muzzle. It came away with a smear of gold. A smile curled his lips.

Daisy had loaded the two gold bullets into the derringer and used them on Aiken.

Slocum tucked the derringer into his coat pocket before looking around. He studied the floor in the kneehole of the desk and saw a plank out of place. Prying it up, Slocum looked down into a large, empty box. He got out his tin of lucifers, struck one and held it close to better examine the box under the flooring. A tiny scrap of paper caught his attention. Slocum pulled it loose from where it was wedged.

Slocum looked at the triangular piece of torn paper and immediately recognized it as the corner of a fifty-dollar bill. A quick reexamination confirmed his first glance. The box was empty. But it had probably held a considerable amount of money not too long ago.

"Burn in hell," Slocum said, getting to his feet and glaring at Aiken. He wished he had been the one pulling the trigger, but before the body was discovered he had to be sure Daisy got out of town.

Slocum made his way outside into what was now a nasty storm, pulled the door closed and saw that the woman's footprints were already filled with snow. There'd be a full-scale blizzard before too much longer. He sighted along the line of disappearing footprints and frowned. It looked as if Daisy went back to the Sweetwater Saloon.

He pulled up his collar to keep the snow from working its way down his neck and trooped the short distance down the street to the saloon. It wasn't possible for everyone in town to be here, but it seemed that way. Loud cries of joy came from inside. Slocum forced his way through the crowd, jumped onto the bar and got a good view of Daisy sitting at a table, a large carpetbag open on the floor beside her.

"Come on up, gentlemen," she said. "I'm buying up all the stock certificates in the Mother Lode Mine you care to sell."

It took the better part of an hour before Daisy ran

through all the money she had taken from under Aiken's floor. She stood and made her way to the door where Slocum met her.

"You want this?" he asked, holding the derringer in the palm of his hand.

"I'm finished with that," Daisy said solemnly. "And I've made what amends I can."

"We'd better leave town fast. When the snowstorm's over, they'll find the body."

Daisy shrugged.

"I don't care. What will they do to me?"

Slocum considered the matter and knew she was right. The prospectors and townspeople who had been bilked out of money buying stock in the bogus claims wouldn't press the matter of a prominent man's death. If anything, they'd think they had been saved the trouble of stringing up Aiken. But Slocum still worried. All it took was one man—whoever the new marshal might be—with a sense of duty to make matters mighty hot for Daisy.

"Let's go back to your cabin. We can leave in the morning, after the storm's over."

Daisy smiled a little more, then asked, "Whatever can we do until morning?"

"We'll find something to do," he assured her. Slocum put his arm around her to protect the woman from the storm, and they left the rowdy, drunken miners to their celebration at having sold their worthless stock certificates.

Watch for

**SLOCUM AND THE BOSS'S WIFE**

325th novel in the exciting SLOCUM series
from Jove

*Coming in March!*